Liberty 2041

episode I

Conceived & Written By

Carolyn & Robert Gold

2020

Series Summary: As an authoritative regime takes over the Earth to halt the rapid advancement of teens, an uprising occurs to repair the world.

Episode Summary: When The Chancellor announces that teens will be severed from their computer enhancements, Jessica copes as the resistance begins. As her ideas take shape, we discover several of the characters, their gifts as well as their fears.

Distribution by KDP- Amazon and Ingram Spark

P.O.D.

Printed in the United States of America and Canada

Title: Liberty 2041

Names: Carolyn Gold and Robert Gold - authors

thegoldtouch.net & liberty2041.com

ISBN: 978-1-952998-00-3 (print)
ISBN: 978-1-952998-01-0 (e-book)

[1. Computers — Fiction 2. Nanotechnology — Fiction 3. Expansive Intelligence — Fiction 4. Intellitela and Glåsse (devices) — Fiction 5. Scarsdale, N.Y. (Town) — Fiction]

Published with Talk+Tell
www.talkplustell.com

To children of all ages …

May you always retain your sense of wonder.

May you find ways to nurture your soul.

May you find daily reasons to smile.

May you live bathed in light.

Life-Altering Technology
Closer Than Ever

Dwelling In A New World
reconstructs communication in every sense.
Author/Inventor, Robert Gold walks us through his
clear understanding of an existence where we
can gain awareness and a direct connection to
safety, kindness, ethics, truth, beauty, and peace.
What was once a futuristic vision of a reimagined
world, is our new reality in the making.
Relationships, both personal and in business are
becoming simpler, more natural and intuitive.

~ Robert Gold,
Dwelling In A New World:
Revealing a Life-Altering Technology, 2012

Table of Contents

spheres. 1

tears 45

fears 86

years 131

Cast 181

Acknowledgments 182

About the Authors 190

spheres

"I'd be so impressed if once, just once, you'd write something with a hopeful tone from beginning to end. You tend to veer off and go in a completely different direction on every single assignment. Why must you always go off course and veer towards controversy?"

"But I thought you liked my alternate views on debatable subjects and the use of multi syllabics?" I responded.

"Yes, I do like your work Jessica . . . for the most part. Being an overthinking planner and strategist are some of your greatest gifts." Mrs. García offered.

Grrr ... If she only knew how I hate being called 'gifted.' First of all, I don't like labels, it's isolating, and that word, in particular, really triggers me. Second, it sounds as if I'm not enough the way I am. As if I needed to be awarded something to succeed. As if I'm not capable on my own.

Mrs. G continues, "I understand that this is how, as the captain of a debate team, a star prosecutor and avid chess player, you get your strategies in order."

"Right, exactly!" I interrupt.

She indicates by her eyebrows coming together that she wasn't quite finished speaking. "I know you're a fast thinker, and perhaps you fear that if you don't write things down or say them the instant they come, you won't remember them later. You feel it's very important that you get your point across. Am I right?"

"Yes! It's that adrenaline rush!" I cut in again, wondering how she could possibly know this about me.

"Believe me. I get you. At your age, I was exactly the same. That's one of the many reasons I became a teacher."

We laugh together. I feel a sense of relief.

Mrs. G becomes serious again. "However, I'd prefer if you didn't use my English Lit class to create the blueprints for your arguments and closing statements."

She's totally on to me. So much for using that approach to process all the stuff that bounces around in my head. How can I turn this around? I need her class. It's better than any therapy I've had to take.

"Thank you for sharing, Mrs. G, so that means you also get how my writing helps so many kids, right?"

"Yes, I do, and that's why I want to continue helping by helping you first. What you went through less than a year ago, at the debate, has taken a tremendous toll on you. I've known you for many years and care about you and that brilliant mind of yours. You need to take a break. Trust me, the world's problems will still be there, waiting for you. In the meantime, for next week's assignment, you must agree, no detours, no controversy, no politics."

"But …!"

"You see this as a challenge, but it's really a great opportunity to write something light and uplifting. I'm giving you a wonderful word I invented. It will help you get inspired. The word is 'cleverty.' Got it?" She says with a quizzical smile.

"Yes, got it, and thank you for the word," I respond, seemingly appreciative, but not happy, not happy at all.

"I expect to learn about your world, but not your inner world. Look outside of yourself in a literal sense. Open a window, take a deep breath, appreciate nature. Discover what's out there instead of being stuck in there all the time." She says, pointing at my head and looking straight into my eyes.

"Understood, dear girl?"

"Yes, ma'am. I absolutely love everything about trees."

"Wonderful! See? You're well on your way! See you next Friday as usual for our in-person meeting in the school building."

Unfortunately, Mrs. G pushed all kinds of buttons with that one brief conversation. I hate being told what to do, it makes me lose my temper, and when that happens, it's not pretty, not pretty at all. My arrogance has never worked well in school, but it sure comes in handy during debates and mock trials. That's where I met Maarlee McGee. We hit it off as we dug deep into the effects of the high expectations imposed upon us superhumans. Living with that pressure every day has definitely added to my already sassy disposition. Now it turns out adults aren't so happy with us after all. The World Chancellor has decided to refer to us as Hybrids, and it's not meant as a compliment.

In retrospect, I'm so grateful Mrs. G took the time to talk to me on Friday. I'm starting to realize that 'my so-called gifts' are also my obstacles. My brain is always turning and churning, so I'm never totally present in the moment. I not only tend to veer off subjects, but I also miss out on experiences happening in real-time right in front of me. Why am I so focused on the future all the time? Why can't I just dive into an experience through art, for example, like Jazz, my best friend who lives across the street. Jazz dances and sings, she paints and does all kinds of crafts. She loves the hair and makeup thing and clothes. Does she ever love clothes!

My eyes close as I go deeper into my famous musings. Why am I the way I am? Why can't I pretend to be shallow and superficial, if just for a day or even a moment? Maybe that would give my brain a break.

I snap back to reality as I hear the sounds of my parents' voices echo through our small two-story house. It feels like I'm living in a shoebox that shakes anytime my obnoxiously loud older brother Jake, speaks. Amazing that despite his thunderous voice, I still managed to doze off for a whole hour and missed breakfast again. I always have snacks stashed away just in case I miss a meal, which happens all the time.

My room is my world. It has everything I need. It's my safe place in spite of the creaky wood floors and a couple of very small windows that fortunately aren't painted shut like the ones in the living room.

I reach for my 'do it all/know it all' communication device resting on that ugly, stained, broken down, much too small hand-me-down nightstand. The Intellitela is my portable instrument that works within an intuitive system. It provides exactly what I need when I need it. And what I need right now is help remaining focused, so I can do my homework.

Ahh … That song is perfectly perfect for background music. While looking out the window to the left of my bed, the idea of what I want to write and the title come quickly. I dictate … Light, Beauty, and Silence By Jessica Stafford. Amazing how well I can function when my body and my mind are entirely in sync.

This title should be positive-sounding enough for Mrs. G. Now, what do I do for the content? Jazz's thoughts on why trees don't make sounds are so inspiring, I've wanted to find an opportunity to use her ideas somehow. Could I be sued for plagiarism for using someone's stream of consciousness?

My thoughts bounce around from homework to plagiarism until I find a safe landing pad on my favorite wall, the one that's directly across from my bed. My whole room is painted a soothing shade of blue-green, but this wall is completely different. There, before me is a wall to wall, floor to ceiling tech wonderland. To think it's already been two years since I got this incredible system which expands the Intellitela's capabilities. Not everyone is lucky enough to have this version, but Jazz and I both do. It enhances any kind of project, and it integrates emotions and sensations with our body. I was so proud the day I was able to explain it all to my parents. Since I'm such a methodical thinker, setting up the wall was rather simple, all I had to do was follow the steps. For many adults, it's been hard to understand, but for those of us who learned how to sync when we were around six-years-old, it's intuitive.

"Okay? Ready?" I instruct with a condescending tone. "Mom, Dad, sit on the bed and look straight ahead."

They smile, take off their shoes, and slide all the way back, leaning against my old headboard. Dad puts his arm behind Mom as if they're going to watch a film. Jake, The Jock, sticks his head in the door. "Is this important enough for me to go get some popcorn?"

He stands by the door impatiently, waiting for a reaction that never comes. My parents know when it's better to ignore him. He rolls his eyes with annoyance, turns around, and leaves.

I try to lighten the mood by saying, "Thank you, Jake Stafford, for that highly anticipated cameo appearance." I clear my throat to regain my audience's attention.

"Ladies and gentlemen, thank you for being here today to learn all about the latest advances in neuroscientific technology. For those of you not familiar with this type of tech, I'll be glad to explain it in simple terms," I say, with a professional tone. The wall activates.

"Oh my, isn't that simply gorgeous?" Mom gushes.

"This may look like a large sheath of glass to the uneducated eye, but in reality, it's made of graphene, a highly malleable and versatile material. It comes packaged as a giant roll, and it adheres on contact with a vertical surface. The translucent spheres you see in various colors and sizes are programmed to move at any speed and direction one chooses. I decided to have them glide across the entire surface of the Glåsse in a liquid-like motion. Some of the spheres are simply decorative, while others labeled like this one, are cells containing messages and conversations from people I already know." I pause and look at my audience to make sure they're following.

"The much larger deep blue-gray globes positioned around the perimeter are stationary. Their function is to store large amounts of personal data, like schoolwork, medical records, social activities, etc. Think of them like heavy file cabinets that you can't move around but can be easily accessed as the data is shared with others."

"So far, so good?" I ask.

They nod and smile ear to ear with pride.

"As you know, I'm not the most imaginative person in an artistic kind of way like Jazz, so it took a lot more thought to assign specific colors to each element based on its function. It took even longer to come up with colors for each of my friends' spheres. I decided to base it on their personality."

"... Or lack thereof." Mom chuckles knowingly.

I turn and give Mom a look and continue speaking. "You'll notice that some spheres are labeled but

9

remain colorless because … well, frankly, I just can't figure that person out."

Mom leans over towards Dad and whispers, "Bet she means Tomas."

"Mooom, I was trying to be professionally discrete!" I stomp my foot, adding still another creak to my floor.

"Sorry." She mouths, pretending to be serious, but not really.

It seems my audience is losing interest after only thirty minutes, so I decide to close my grand presentation sooner than expected.

"Mom, Dad, thank you for knowing me so well and giving me the best instruments possible to continue developing as an enhanced human. This expanded version of Glåsse, which operates with the handheld Intellitela, is beyond because it spreads across my entire wall. It's more than I could have ever imagined. I can do homework, conduct business, and communicate with my friends in different ways I haven't even discovered yet."

I jump on the bed to join them. We hear a crack and then a snap. Had I only jumped a little harder, we would have ended up on the floor, which would have been an excellent thing. Maybe then

I could finally get something suitable for my age. This was Mom's childhood set; it remains indestructible no matter what I do to it. She calls it 'good quality' while I call it 'give it up and let me grow up.'

Dad responds, "You're welcome, Princessa; after all, it is 2039. It's not every day that our daughter turns twelve. You work very hard at everything you do; you deserve the best we can give you."

Bam! The whole house vibrates. Jake had been eavesdropping the whole time and chose to express his jealous frustration by slamming his door as hard as he could. It made his old iron door knob clunk down on the floor. To distract my parents, I cheer them up by sharing one last detail. "Mom, Dad, I almost forgot, while I was learning about all the Glåsse modalities, I discovered that by keeping the spherical dance going 24/7, I feel much more relaxed."

"That's the best part of this entire presentation, sweetie," Mom says, as Dad catches her happy tears with his fingers.

"It's a known fact that adults are struggling with some parts of modern technology. Would you say this presentation was slightly over your heads? Did you learn anything new?" I ask arrogantly.

They laugh but only slightly amused.

"Did you feel you knew more about technology than your parents?"

Dad chuckles, "We definitely knew we were way ahead of our parents just like you feel about us right now. We also thought we were ahead of our young children, but that changed once The Implants For All Initiative went into effect."

"This has been a huge leap for everyone, even for your Dad, who's been in tech development forever." Mom states.

"Was it hard to accept that your kids were getting nano implants and would become superhumans?"

Mom smiled gently, "Let's just say that in our case, we welcomed it because we had rather intense children ..."

"Since birth," Dad interjects.

Mom gives him a disapproving look and continues, "We saw you both struggling in some areas like not being able to remain focused, not having much patience and resisting when being told what to do. We knew these traits were crucial for a developing child, and we wanted to give our children every advantage possible to excel. We thought that even if we started you a little later, you were six, and Jake was eight, the nano implants would still be helpful as you got older. But, initially, we felt rather …"

"Well, got to get back to work! That was an excellent presentation, Jess." Dad cuts in, jumping up.

Mom hugs me gently while Dad kisses me on the head. They reach for their shoes and walk out holding hands, their next stop, Jake's room. Instinctively I raise the music's volume to drown out the arguing.

Later on, I joined Mom downstairs to help fix dinner. As usual, she acts as if everything is okay, and nothing has happened. I asked her why Dad cuts in so abruptly while others are speaking. "Mom, he does it to you; it's awful. I do it too. It's not very polite, is it?" I say, feeling ashamed.

"Glad you're starting to notice these things, you're growing up. Some people have so much to say that they're afraid that if they don't get it out at that moment, something awful will happen."

"Exactly, what I have to say is very important; if I don't get it out, I'll explode like a balloon, and my hair will land on the floor like a mop!"

Mom and I burst out laughing at the absurdity of the image.

"Jess, being superhuman, gives you a unique opportunity to improve on your parents' actions. With or without nano implants, we have to realize that we're all still human and have frailties."

Two years have passed since that conversation. Here I am at age fourteen, still trying to work on myself not to be rude to people. Life is hard having to think about others and juggle one's own adolescent emotions. The nanos and supportive systems have made it easier for us kids. So in honor of Mrs. G's request, I'll make an effort to remain positive and patient today. There's enough negativity out there; I don't need to add to it.

I dictate, "Today, I'm not going to let anything or anyone get under my skin. I will start looking for light and beauty."

Speaking of beauty ... a sphere, in the palest of pinks, drifts gently onto my wall. It's Jazz!

"*Bonjour,* what are you doing on this cold, dreary day?"

"Whatever it is, trust me, it's happening under these covers."

Jazz laughs her wonderful laugh and shifts gracefully to another matter, "I just heard from Tomas, he's very agitated this morning. The WLC is getting ready to broadcast shortly."

"Tomas is always agitated. What set him off this time? To think I had such high hopes for today." I mumble sarcastically.

"Jess, his agitation feels different to me; it's really serious. Please be open-minded about Tomas; he's a good guy, and he's well connected to people and information we know nothing about."

Jazz is looking straight at me from her bedroom window across the street. Her arms cross, and she gives me 'the look.'

As we continue to analyze the many reasons why Tomas gets so easily upset, I need to interrupt.

"It's only 10:30 in the morning, why is it getting dark outside?"

Jazz makes overly theatrical Shakespearian hand gestures.

"Farewell, my muse, my beloved. I beg thee, do not drift away, for the morn is still young." She recites with a polished British accent and then blows a kiss in the air.

I applaud, "That was lovely, Mademoiselle Rossé. Are you in the middle of the English Lit assignment too?" I giggle.

"Indeed, I am m' lady." She bows gracefully.

"Do you like my Ode to Light and Beauty?" She says, maintaining her regal accent.

That's wild … Did I pick up on her idea for the title of our assignment, or did she pick up on mine? Is that plagiarism or telepathy?

"You are so good at everything you do, Jazz".

"Thank you, Jess, that's so nice of you."

"If I didn't like you so much … I would …" I catch myself, but it's too late.

Bleep!

How did my jealousy and insecurity surface like that? Why didn't my sensors warn me ahead of time?

"If you didn't like me so much, what … Jessica Stafford?" She asks defiantly.

Oh no, now I've upset her. How could I be so thoughtless? I hate seeing my best friend sad. She's always upbeat and rarely upset. I wonder if that's what makes her flawless almond toned skin glow the way it does. And those mounds of curly cinnamon hair, the way they move so gracefully when she walks. I may not be artistic like she is, but I can appreciate the artistry of her look and her demeanor. So lucky we met when we were infants on the day the Ross's decided

16

to buy the house across the street. Our parents became fast friends on the spot.

"You've hurt my feelings." Jazz says, crying.

"I know, it wasn't intentional, really. You know how I feel about you, and you know how my mood changes with the light and the barometric pressure, and —."

"Those aren't valid excuses, and you know it." She snaps, stomping her foot on the floor.

"Jazz, please forgive me."

This is all so weird. Usually, Jazz is so together and mature; my comments don't tend to affect her like this. I can hear her little bunny rabbit sniffles as she pulls back the tears.

I change the subject to something superficial, not my style, at all.

"Do you know if we're expecting a storm or an eclipse? Look at it."

She finally speaks. "I don't think so. Look at that murky looking stuff heading this way. I can even taste it coming through the vents in my room. Yuck. There's no way this could be industrial pollution. We don't live anywhere near any manufacturing plants. What's this grody looking stuff?" She asks nervously and starts coughing.

Looking up at the sky, I realize the sun is gone. I can't see Jazz anymore either, and that makes me anxious. What's going on?

I unlock the window latch as Jazz is trying to stay with me through the coughing. "I'm a woman of science, so I need to get answers."

"I can hear you. Stop, don't do it! What if it's not pollution at all, what if it's a poisonous gas attack!" She's coughing and gasping.

I ignore her comment completely, raise the window all the way, pushing my whole upper body out the window.

"Ugh ... disgusting! The air smells and tastes putrid. It's not cold or warm. It's like there's no temperature at all." I shout out as if my voice could cut through the stuff. I pull myself back in and slam the window. Blowing my nose is the only thing I can think of to get rid of the awful taste. I hop back into the safety of my bed and cover up. "Well, so much for that nasty little adventure. I have no idea what's going on. So where were we Jazz? Oh yeah, figuring out what's bothering Tomas Kesher this morning."

Jazz says nothing, she's gasping for air. I hope her lung issues don't kick in again because of this. She ended up in the clinic last time.

"Jess, I can't —." She coughs some more, and then the sound cuts off.

I turn to look at my Glåsse and — Nooo! … my beautiful spheres are getting flattened against the perimeter of the wall. I check the controls on the keyboard and nothing's working, they're locked.

"Oh, c'mon, not today. Jazz … Jazz? Can you hear me?" I plead.

My anxiety level is rising. I need to see Jazz, and I need my spheres! Why isn't anything working right today? In my desperation, I remember to look up at my tranquil ceiling. It's set up to respond when I'm lying down in bed. I find slow-moving images from the Hubble very soothing.

Nooo … that's fading too! Every surface of my room is becoming a sickly pasty gray. It's making me feel physically ill.

First Jazz, then the spheres, then the ceiling and now the ambient light is gone too? I let out a scream.

My room looks and feels just like I do … horrible!

I'm having a full-blown anxiety attack, the same way I feel when I see …

Oh please nooo — The World Chancellor's unmistakable silhouette is materializing on my wall. His presence generates that same sickly pasty gray sensation if I'm not fully prepared to deal with him.

"This is not good, not good at all," I say, trembling.

I keep tapping mute, delete, refresh, nothing happens. The gray silhouette on the wall starts to get darker and more substantial. In a matter of seconds, it transforms into a life-size hologram. He looks right and left, takes a step away from the wall and appears to be standing at the foot of my bed.

"Stop!" I scream.

He raises one eyebrow and seems to be leering at me.

"World leaders, we are gathered here today to address the most serious threat to humanity since The Global Depression two decades ago. In recent weeks, we've investigated the actions and witnessed the ramifications of our enemies' reactive behavior. They have grown powerful through acts of defiance and violence."

Wait ... who's he talking to? I thought he was at The WLC, but no one else is visible. Is he really there, or is he at a studio? Forget it, that wouldn't work for him. He craves live audiences. He concealed everyone around him so he could be the center of attention ... as always.

He pauses and leans in. "Are we willing to wait to find out what The Hybrids are capable of doing next, now that they have infiltrated our most sophisticated technology? I say absolutely not!" He shouts so loudly that my old windows rattle.

He adds a sense of urgency to his voice and continues, "Their rebellious nature can no longer be ignored nor tolerated. Their capacity to organize rapidly is disrupting peacekeeping missions around the globe. Therefore, we have no choice but to make radical changes in our laws."

"Gentlemen, the world is in imminent danger, and if we don't act immediately, I fear for our future. We cannot allow them to take over the world." He roars with an exaggerated *vibrato*.

"The Hybrids are not only ungrateful, but they are also highly dangerous subhumans. Parents, be warned, for your own good, do not trust your children. I repeat, do not trust your children. I urge you to refer to the original manuals and review the nano implants' original intentions. Be vigilant and beware of who they have become. Through reliable sources, we know they are modifying all their nanos and misusing them for nefarious purposes."

What is he talking about? Imminent danger? Subhumans and Hybrids? My thoughts are spinning out of control. How dare he label us and talk about us in such demeaning terms? What have we done to deserve this? We're just kids trying to have a better future. Is he so upset because the whole plan backfired? Because we surpassed the adult's expectations? Is that why this monster was elected to get rid of us? We see him for who he is, a manipulative, narcissistic, lying monster; he's making us the villains by turning it all on us and creating mass hysteria. I've studied about people like him in anthropology, psychology, and history journals. He fits the dictator profile to a T. He has no empathy. He doesn't know how to spell the word. I think he's mad because we're messing with his plans for world domination. Well, too bad because it's too late, we won't be stopped!

He's warning adults not to trust us when we have good reasons not to trust them. Everyone, between thirteen and fifteen, no matter where we live on the planet, has similar issues. We have the same resentments towards adults because they continue leaving the next generation holding the ball with a messed up world. Is it too much to ask that they help their own kids and grandkids? Why don't they care, and why haven't they figured out how to function as a society without armaments?

We're so tired of violence, but thanks to adults who set the example, that's all we know. Why are they so surprised by all the uprisings? Despite all the greed, corruption, and pollution that aims to destroy everything in its path, here we are, fewer than before and surrounded by the little bit of nature we still have. It's a miracle this ancient planet is still around.

"I hate you!" I repeat over and over as I punch pillows one by one all over the room.

An invisible entity must be saying something to him because he pauses for a few seconds. He turns again from side to side to make sure he has everyone's full attention as he glances at some papers?

Paper? In 2041? Do we need any more proof that he's also an ecological ignoramus?

"We must unite and stop the subhumans in their tracks. We must have a unanimous vote to disable their nano implants immediately. Therefore, at the conclusion of this announcement, you will be given extensive documentation for your review detailing the current nanos and those introduced during the last eight years. Each world leader has been assigned a private cubicle in the interior of this building, where they shall remain in isolation until further notice. We have instituted the strictest security measures to guarantee zero distractions during this arduous task."

"Silence!"

The sound in the auditorium is shut off, but clearly, the voiceless crowd is protesting. We'll never know who dared defy him.

He continues to growl, "All devices belonging to the council were confiscated this morning to attend this meeting. They shall remain in custody until further notice."

"Silence, Silence!" He yells.

"As a courtesy, we plan to serve meals and beverages. You may eat and drink what we provide when we provide it. Should it not meet your cultural or dietary needs, you may fast."

"Silence, Silence, Silence!" He tries to yell even louder.

"Be forewarned that our loyal staff has been instructed not to speak nor listen to anyone nor provide any type of assistance. Any deviation of this mandate will be dealt with accordingly. Official escorts will be made available for personal breaks after the meal."

Are you kidding me? That's not a loyal staff! They're brainwashed zombies. He isn't even allowing world leaders to go to the bathroom alone? What could they possibly do? What is he so afraid of?

"Silence, I say!" The Chancellor demands.

"You're an absolutely 100% incompetent wacko crazy subhuman yourself!" I scream and throw my last pillow at the hologram.

"No one under the age of eighteen will have implants going forward. All hospitals around the world are being notified at this very moment not to implant any new offspring as of midnight tonight. We have decided to roll back the clock eight years for our collective safety."

"Silence, I say!"

He pauses to take a drink from what looks like a medieval goblet. If only someone would dare slip a magic potion into his beverage to make him disappear. Then, we could roll back the clock to a time of safety and sanity.

"What's happening to my wall now?"

A red flashing box appears directly over his head, black letters starting to form inside. The last thing I need right now is to see red flashing anything. That's the color that alerts me when I'm in emotional upheaval.

When the letters are no longer blurred, the sign reads:

> **HYBRID DEACTIVATION SERVICES**
> **< EFFECTIVE IMMEDIATELY >**
> **AGES EIGHTEEN & UNDER**
>
> Upgraded implantation Program
> Center Supervised Recalibration
>
> **DEACTIVATION DATE TO BE ANNOUNCED**

"What are you trying to do to us, you heartless monster?" I scream loudly.

"Ouch, I think I've just ripped something in my throat."

"Silence! Silence!" The Chancellor demands.

In the next room, Jake is screaming, cursing, slamming things furiously. There's a long pause and then ... Crash! It sounds like he just threw something through his closed window. I cover my ears and start rocking. My heart is beating like crazy, my head, fingers, and toes are throbbing all at once. Please let this be a horrible nightmare. Even under the covers, I can still hear everything. Please, please make it go away.

"Mommy ... Where's my mommy?" I cry out.

He goes on to say, "When we reconvene later today at 3:00 PM, I expect a unanimous vote whether leaders are physically present or in another country. The next session is closed to the public."

He stops speaking and leans to one side as the invisible entity speaks to him. He seems enraged.

"I've just been informed that under current law, the session must be open to the public. But Evil Hybrids, don't you dare try anything that will endanger the safety and life of others. This building and a considerable radius are already under heavy surveillance. We will be adding one final law to our roster; as of tomorrow morning, no more public attendance on votes." He looks both ways and announces, "Gentlemen, this session is adjourned!"

He looks both ways and takes a step back. The hologram reverses, and the small flat gray silhouette goes … poof! If only it were that easy to get rid of him.

Is it over? A moment longer would have been unbearable. I go into hyperdrive to process what just happened.

The World Chancellor has taken over all forms of communication. He's erased everyone's image and sounds in the auditorium other than his. He sequestered hundreds of foreign dignitaries and will not allow them even to go to the bathroom alone. His message to our parents is not to trust us, well now you've proven we can't trust adults either.

Why did he keep saying gentlemen even though we all know there were women dignitaries? I gather that for him, women and children and trees shouldn't be part of his planet, only subservient men. Something catches my eye and makes me look outside. It's the sun trying to come back!

I look at the time and exclaim, "Whaat? It's noon already?" Ninety minutes of unbearable torture? He took over my body, my emotions, and my room turning everything into the color I despise the most.

Ahh … just in time, my ambient light is working again. Things are starting to look back to normal, except for my wall. Instead of peaceful spheres, I have hundreds of tiny amoeba-shaped objects moving frantically and bumping into each other while others are sticking. The wall is in complete chaos, and so am I. All I can do is cry.

A sapphire blue sphere appears with the familiar aquatic glide, appeasing the frantic amoebas.

"Jess, it's me, can you hear me? Are you okay?"

"… I'm… so … glad … to … see …you …" I say sobbing with relief.

"I've never seen you ... quite like this before." Josef says, studying me intently. Then he smiles his smile.

"I know you have sphere issues, so stay focused on me, got it?"

I nod with what I imagine is a puzzled grin of total delight — no problem focusing just on him right now. Look at how he looks when he looks at me; that square jawline and cleft chin, that thick wavy blonde hair. I stare while imagining tomorrow's feed headline.

BREAKING NEWS

Ms. Jessica Stafford, Scarsdale media sensation, publicly admits, "I'm just a typical teenager. Staring into Junior Officer Josef Tallon-Saldane's blue eyes made me forget that the world is about to come to an end."

Stand by for updates on this developing story.

I come back to reality when Josef asks, "Are you sick, what happened to your voice?"

"No, I just feel sick from what we just witnessed. I've been screaming at the wall for the last ninety minutes." I say, somewhat embarrassed.

"Do you want me to come over, Jess? We need to be together right now. I think it's important."

"Believe me, there's nothing I'd love more than for you to come over, but my family is at war. There's been yelling and screaming nonstop for days now. Jake was in big trouble already, but after what just happened, he'll be in trouble for years."

"Why? What happened?"

"Well, you already know about Jake's incident with the law in Manhattan last December, right? Well, today, he outdid himself. From the sound of it, I think he destroyed his entire bedroom and then threw something through his window."

"Oh man, that's crazy. The announcement set him off, right? Where are your parents right now?"

I space out wondering why Jake and I both have so much rage.

He repeats, "Jess, where are your parents?"

"Oh, sorry, no idea." I say, realizing the house is completely quiet.

"I miss seeing you in person. It's been way too long. How about we meet at the coffee shop across from the railroad station?" Josef shares.

"Are you showing up on a white stallion to rescue me from The Ogre?"

Surprisingly, I'm okay with Josef seeing me being totally vulnerable like this.

"I shall prepare my white stallion and arrive post-haste. I look forward to seeing the damsel no longer in distress."

"I feel better already; thank you for checking on me."

"Of course! Shall we say in ... forty-five then?" He asks.

"I'm eager to see thy countenance," I reply.

"You have English Lit homework this week, too?" He chuckles.

Managing a nod and a weak smile, I say, "Bye." His beautiful sapphire sphere drifts off. I can finally exhale. I collapse on the bed, feeling physically and emotionally wiped out.

"Mirror", I command. The Intellitela reveals the terrible truth.

"Oh, nooo ... please ... nooo!" I scream in horror. This is beyond terrible. One thing is to let him see my vulnerability, but this! He saw a panoramic view of my tornadic room and my tangled, mangled hair.

Wow, he must really like me if he wants to meet, even if I look like I've been in a wind tunnel.

Dreamy eyed and a bit shell shocked, I sit up in bed, facing Jazz's window. Glad I can see her again, she looks absorbed in her work, I won't disturb her. I do love her, hope she knows it, I've never told her. It was scary when she started coughing and we lost contact earlier.

I reach for the natural bristle brush that lives in the tiny top drawer of my small nightstand. There's something to be said about the calming feeling I get from this low-tech sensory tool my mom has used on me since I was a little girl. The hair and body brushing have always had a soothing effect on me. That's one thing I won't ever let go of, no matter my age.

Looking at the brush, I say out loud, "It's time my bedroom and my body start looking my age. Would you agree, Mrs. Brush?" I smile, remembering the day we named 'her' years ago.

As I start to untangle my messy mane, I remember that once upon a time, all I was known for was my hair and nothing else. I was Jessica, the petite girl with the big personality and industrial quantities of dark mahogany hair. Looking at the nightstand, I practice the same conversation I've had in my head over and over again.

"Mom, we need to talk about my furniture. I'm fourteen and not your Baby Girl anymore."

Then I imagine her crying, and that ends the talk.

Okay, hair's done, ready to face the world, the cold air will do wonders for me. With renewed energy, I get dressed and gallop rhythmically downstairs wearing my beat up, but ever so comfortable winter boots. Before grabbing my heavy jacket, knit cap, and gloves from the front closet, I see my parents and Jake sitting in the living room, all looking very somber, not moving or speaking. They look up when I clear my throat. The tension is as thick as the brown murk from this morning. The arguing may have stopped, but we all know it's only a truce.

"I'm going to the village for a bit to catch up with Josef. I'll be back before dinner. Can I get you anything, Mom? Maybe your favorite French pastries from the bakery? Dad, any last-minute building supplies you might need from the hardware store? Jake, a passport application?"

Dad and Jake give me dirty looks, guess family humor has its limits. Mom awakens from her daze and offers a delayed robotic response. "Thank you, sweetie, nothing, we're fine. Say hi to Josef. Have a good time." She says, smiling.

We're fine … Seriously? Our home and the world are collapsing, and she thinks we're fine? What's wrong with her? As long as we eat meals together and on time, all else can fall by the wayside.

I open the front door and feel the cold air on my face. Just as I'm about to look up the term denial, Maarlee McGee's vibrant pineapple yellow sphere glides in.

"*Aloha!* How's your day been so far?" She says tongue in cheek.

"Just peachy. Yours?" I reply.

"Hard to grasp what's around the corner for us, huh?" Her tone lacks its usual joyful luster.

"How did we get ourselves into this, Maar? I'm still in a bit of daze and don't know what to think."

"You think we got ourselves into this?" Maarlee sounds surprised.

"Well, that's what I'm trying to sort out. We were 'conceived' to be the generation that would right all the wrongs of the world."

"And the concept sounded so impressive that it made our parents hopeful," Maarlee adds.

"Well, yeah, imagine the deal they were about to get. Those of us born after 2025 were going to clean up the gigantic mess the previous generations left behind. Who wouldn't accept and sign on the dotted line? Install the best technology available in our children; in fact, the more, the better." I say with a hefty dose of sarcasm.

"I never thought of it quite that way before," Maar says.

"Think of it, once we started implementing our knowledge and strengths, everything shifted," I explain.

"What do you mean, shifted?" She inquires.

"Well, we went from being pampered and revered to becoming an international threat to society pretty much overnight."

Maarlee's silence puts me in full mock trial mode, "So, ladies and gentlemen of the jury, I ask you ... Are kids responsible in any way for allowing things to reach this level of discord? Can kids under the age of eighteen override public opinion and change how adults perceive them despite the heavy propaganda against them?"

My smart friend takes a deep breath before responding, "I honestly don't see how we're responsible for any of this, what you're saying sounds plain crazy. Don't forget that none of the enhancements and nano implants were our choice to begin with. So please, Jess, don't even go there. We didn't get ourselves into anything."

"You're right, they designed us to be different, so why should we take the blame for it now. Who came up with that term, Hybrids, anyway? It's so demeaning."

"I'm sure a member of his cabinet who gets paid lots of money to be clever with words. Their use and what comes once the terms are out in the public domain are no longer their concern. Sound bites will forever reign as long as the world is round."

"Since sound bytes will reign forever, we need to flood the media with positivity. I just need to figure out how."

As I say that, I'm getting a little nervous discussing these things in such detail with her. We all know that The World Leadership Conference is supposed to be monitoring everything we do and say. For some reason, Maarlee seems to be exempt from that scrutiny.

"Let's talk about this sensibly," she suggests.

"The Implants For All Initiative was designed to benefit children and adults. It took a lot less time for our age group to get accustomed to things. Six-year-olds adjust more easily to change, and then it becomes perfectly natural. For adults who were used to living with externals only, this whole thing has been much more difficult. I think they're still adjusting, I see it in my parents. They're so awkward with it. We dance with it."

"That's it! I just realized something, natural vs. unnatural. The way our parents are reacting or not reacting to all of this is completely unnatural. It's like they're just standing by, watching while we're treated like things. Why aren't they more upset? Why aren't they protesting these injustices with us?"

"I think adults are just as scared as we are. They're afraid that if we continue to protest, things will get worse for everyone, that's why they don't want us to get more out of control."

"C'mon Maar, do you think our parents are willing to see us careen down a spiral of total confusion and despair by losing our implants in exchange for not losing control over us? We're teenagers, that's what we do. We're supposed to get out of control. That's what our parents did. I don't buy it. Something's off!"

"Well, what's your theory, then?"

"I don't have one quite yet, but their lack of action is not typical of parents protecting their children from danger. From where I stand right now, I only trust a handful of adults. The jury is still out on my parents." I snap.

"Jessica Lynn Stafford, you don't mean that, do you?" Maarlee raises her voice.

"No ... well maybe, I guess not, I'm just furious and really confused right now."

The edges of my device are starting to turn deep orange, indicating my temper could escalate.

"Let's not get too worked up over this, you know there's no turning back for you."

"You're right. I'm the infamous and brilliant teenager with an explosive temper. I've never told you this but, you're one of the few people who can follow my train of thought, even when it derails. You always seem to know how to get me back on track. Thank you for that."

"Wow, coming from you that's quite a compliment. You're such a clever wordsmith. I may just hire you to write for my show."

We laugh disproportionately loud because we need to release all the tension we have pent up inside. It's nice to hear ourselves acting like regular giddy teenage girls after such a horrendous morning.

"How's your communication platform coming along lately?" Maar wants to know.

"Liberty World is what keeps me going. Initially, it's where I got material for the debates. Kids are worried about so many issues, and they've chosen me as their spokesperson. Guess, that's why it's growing exponentially, they feel heard, for a change. Everyone that's joined the group is being supportive of one another. So far, no infiltrators or agitators have managed to get in."

"You're doing a great job of keeping them out. That great mission statement of yours, Trust & Unity, and the questionnaire you came up with are beyond excellent. Only those with sincere intentions could jump through that ring of fire."

I should give Jazz all the credit for the mission statement, the questionnaire, and how the platform runs. But selfishly, I say nothing other than, "Thank you, Maar, coming from you, that's quite a compliment."

"You and your group are bound to make a difference because after today, our world is going in reverse." Maarlee sighs deeply.

I deflect my selfish guilt by making myself a victim. "Honestly, I don't know how you manage to be a public figure. To think you choose to be in the spotlight, while I've been thrown into it — not by choice. And all because of what happened after the debate last May."

"So what do you think put you in the spotlight? Was it the statements Senator Kravitz made? Do you feel he's using you to advance his own political agenda?"

"You are such a good interviewer, and usually, you're the voice of reason, but in this case, I disagree with you. I honestly don't think he intended to use me at all; he's sincere and wants the best for all of us; he has teenage daughters and aging parents."

"I have an idea. Would you like to be on my show to explain why you think Senator Kravitz is not taking advantage of our current situation to advance his political agenda? I could easily make that happen." She offers.

"About Senator Kravitz, it's important that everyone knows why he wants to establish voting rights for teens by age fourteen. It's equally important I stay out of the public eye and not make a statement on his behalf. So thank you, Maar, but don't think it's the best thing to do. I'm in enough trouble already."

"Ms. Stafford, you're always full of surprises. I thought you would have jumped at the chance to make a point in public."

"Not anymore," I reply.

Maar starts laughing, "I just had a thought, if I were to write about you, the first paragraph might sound something like this …"

"It all started when a thirteen-year-old girl from Scarsdale, NY, won a debate viewed by over a hundred million people. Much to her surprise, she changed the course of history."

"Wow, that sounds great. You're hired to write my autobiography."

"Great, I accept the challenge! So go and change the world so that I have lots of content for several interviews that will lead to my upcoming award-winning novel."

"Sounds good, but right now, I'm on my way to meet Josef."

"As in the very handsome and accomplished … ?"

"Yup, that would be him." I gush. "Thanks for deprogramming me during our walk, it's been very helpful, and Josef will reap the benefits. I'll be less wound up by the time I get to the village."

"Jess, remember, be in the moment … relax … enjoy."

"*Ciao* for now," I say, knowing that's Jazz's favorite phrase. The pineapple sphere floats out of view. As I get closer to town, the urban colors of street signs, traffic lights, and brick buildings add life to the drab fog and dirty snow.

As I get closer to the train station, seeing the emerald green tile roof gives me a jolt of energy. That's the shade of green I chose as my balance color. When I see it, everything inside me settles down.

My thoughts have a purpose and a direction instead of bouncing around aimlessly. As I spot the coffee shop a few paces away, Josef's beautiful sapphire sphere drifts in on my Intellitela.

"Hey Jess, I'm about ten minutes away."

I'm blushing with anticipation. "Josef, I want you to know how much this means to me, your coming here to see me and all."

"You're very important to me, and today gives me a chance to prove it. I've been worried about how you'd react to the announcement."

My heart is thumping loudly. I'm afraid that he'll hear it on his device.

"Thank you, Josef, you're a special guy."

What I wish I could say is that I like him so much.

Aside from being crazy handsome, he's mature and generous; he goes out of his way to be supportive, reliable, and trustworthy. Wonder if he's that way because he and Stefan grew up under such difficult circumstances? Either way, they're outstanding guys with full scholarships at The Military Academy in Hartsdale.

"Jess?" He says.

"What, sorry?" I respond, coming back from the daze.

"Hold up your Intellitela."

"Why, what's wrong?"

"Just do it, please." He requests.

"Ahh … Much better, I just needed to see you before I saw you."

I respond playfully, "Oh right, you're just making sure I combed my hair since this morning, right?"

"Of course not, but now that you mention it, glad to see you did. See you soon." He chuckles and winks.

My body temperature just rose even though it's 20 degrees and starting to drop, I'm too excited to wait inside, so I keep walking. Since smell is one of my dominant senses, I can't deny myself the healing powers of the scent of hot butter and cinnamon coming from the French bakery. I close my eyes, inhale deeply, and imagine graceful amber shapes swirling all around me.

"We're pulling up," Josef announces. I run towards the cafe.

"Is that you, waving at me with the green gloves and knit cap? It is you!"

"I see you, I see you!" I say, jumping up and down, waving frantically. People are staring, and frankly, I don't care.

What a romantic guy, he made sure to request a white vehicle to make up for not having a white stallion. Time seems to slow down as I watch him get out. Look at him in that full-length thick charcoal gray wool coat with double-breasted shiny gold buttons. The collar is flipped up high around his ears, making his blond hair blow in the cold like golden rays of sun.

I intend to store this moment in my mind for the rest of my life.

tears

Sitting in total silence with Josef while sipping hot chocolate with lots of whipped cream, drizzled with chocolate syrup, is my idea of perfection. Any girl would be more than thrilled to have this tall, strong, handsome guy with the clearest of blue eyes ever, next to her. He's a good listener and can make points with a few words. He's firm when I need it, but he's also caring and considerate. What does he see in me that I don't see in myself? I'm a mega intense, highly opinionated tomboy with a child's body and way too much hair. As I ponder on this mystery, I turn discretely to catch a glimpse of his chiseled jawline and get interrupted.

An urgent signal shows up on the table top's Glåsse. "Not noow!"

"C'mon, not again, another announcement?" I exclaim, hitting the table with my fist.

"Oh wow, now that's great … done!"

"What's going on. What's done?" Josef looks up from his reading.

"It was a notice about today's assembly at the WLC. The last two available seats showed up, so I grabbed them before someone else did."

"And you paid how much for them?" He asks with annoyance.

"They're free. Why do you ask?"

"Never mind, you wouldn't understand." He looks away.

"Try me, you never know, I may surprise you," I say, licking the chocolate syrup off the back of my spoon.

"This is nothing to joke about." He snaps.

"Alright, I'll tell you. The thought that you were spending money instead of spending time with me put me in a bad place. It's a childhood thing I still have to work on."

"I'm truly sorry, Josef. I didn't mean to make light of it. I have noticed that money always seems to bother you in some way or another, and I'd like to understand why."

"Maybe some other time." He replies sternly.

"Whenever you're ready, I'm here."

He gives me an apprehensive look.

"I'm trying to be more aware of other peoples' emotional needs and how they intertwine with mine."

"Really? How?" He asks sarcastically, waiting for me to make a point.

"I realize I've done or said something wrong right after it happens. It's like being a beat behind in a song, like my timing's off. Do you know what I'm trying to say?"

He nods and tilts his head, "Somewhat."

"It's great that the system sensed it was important for me to attend the last WLC meeting that will be open to the public, but it's bad that I didn't consider you in the decision until after it happened. Without nano implants, will we have less capacity to make better decisions?"

"Girls!" He snaps. "I just don't get you. You're all over the place. What's it like living inside your messy heads? Weren't you just starting to settle down from this morning, now you want more and in person?"

I've never seen Josef lose his cool with me like this; it doesn't feel good at all. I now get the expression 'You can dish it out, but you sure can't take it.' He's hurt my feelings for the first time, but I deserve it.

"I had no intention of going, honestly."

He looks at me very seriously, "I spend weeks at a time cooped up with a bunch of dull guys in the dorm. What do you not understand about my wanting to come to town and spend time with you? I didn't come all this way to spend my day with 2800 other highly agitated people in an auditorium."

He looks both mad and disappointed.

"How can I prove to you that I'm sorry?"

"I don't know right now; you always act as if the only feelings that matter are yours." He replies.

"You're right, how do you put up with me? I'm impulsive, irrational, and irritating."

"See? You've unconsciously or unintentionally put the attention back on yourself. Make an effort and stop focusing on how you think others perceive you. It would give you a mental break." He says reassuringly.

"If only I knew how to get out of my own head," I say sadly.

"Jess, I like spending time with you because you're intelligent and inspirational. You think on your feet and get yourself out of almost any jamb. But, man, when you go into overdrive, you don't know when to stop."

I'm starting to get the full picture, he sees me as a smart friend and a diversion from military school. It just so happens I'm a girl. He didn't mention that he wants to be with me because he finds me attractive. Clearly, I'm not. I mean, look at me! I need to research how to control a crush with and without implants before I embarrass myself. From reading so many novels for English Lit class, I know all about heartbreak. I don't ever want to experience that; I'll make sure of it.

"Thank you for the advice, you're right. But in the case of going to the WLC, you and I both know we can't trust The Chancellor nor his grandiose theatrical productions. We need to find out what's going on. We have a chance to witness history in the making, Josef, but I fully understand if you choose not to come with me. I can manage on my own."

Oops, I didn't mean that. Now, what do I do? I know, I'll resort to my little whimpering pouty puppy face, it's irresistible.

"Alright Jess, you win; if it's important to you, it's important to me, I'll go with you." He sounds defeated.

The pouty puppy approach worked once again!

"Really? You'll come with me?"

I clasp my hands together in delight and feel triumphant. A sharp twinge in the back of my right knee and a bleep remind me that what just happened wasn't good, not good at all. I can tell that Josef has shifted from being disappointed to being responsible.

"How could I ever face your parents again if I let you go there alone. It's heavily guarded but by all the wrong people. We're now viewed as targets and *provocateurs*."

"Thank you for being a good friend. Today is not just for me or you, it's for all of us, because our future is in jeopardy." I say, looking deeply into his eyes.

He looks puzzled, "You see me as a good friend?"

"Of course, I do!" I shift gears pretending I'm not disappointed that he's not interested in me as his girlfriend. "If we rush, we can catch the next train into the city; we've got fourteen minutes. I'll race you!" We grab our things and whoosh … he's off.

"I should have known better than to race you," I say, panting as he waits nonchalantly by the entrance.

"That's what happens when you challenge a triathlete." He winks.

We get to the platform, and he goes back to reading 'Variations On Military Ground Formations Volume 3'.

"That looks incredibly boring, is it?"

He shakes his head without looking up.

Does he prefer reading about war strategy over talking to me? But who can blame him, really? It must be exhausting to be with me, I exhaust myself. We're so different in so many ways. I've had an easy life up until recently. I've never known what it's like not to have parents or a permanent home or a bed or toys of my own. He's always had to worry about survival while I seek conflict so I can fight for injustice.

Josef carries himself with such dignity. If only I could be more like him and less like myself.

Josef interrupts as if he could read my thoughts. "What are you thinking about?"

"You caught me thinking of our attributes in case we have a chance to change the world together."

The train pulls up just at the right time. We get on and find seats side by side. Typical me, I blurt out of nowhere, "May I ask you something?"

"Is it about the WLC?"

"No, not exactly, but it's very important."

He stares at me with slight annoyance. I clear my throat and ask, "Would you consider sharing your hue.r.u quotient with me?"

He gets visibly uncomfortable and whispers back sternly. "Never, ever, even if you tortured me with major doses of your irresistible pouty puppy thing. I'm a junior cadet trained to not cave in under pressure. What you're asking for is dangerous and against the law, and you know it."

"Okay, okay — I just thought since it's hard for you to express feelings, I'd get to know you better that way."

"You know you're relentless, don't you?" He quips.

"One of my most endearing qualities," I respond, batting my eyelashes.

Finally … He's leaning over to say something romantic.

"Jess, we must never divulge any part of our quotient to anyone, especially now. Understand?"

My hopes deflate …

He continues, "We don't know who or what is listening. The laws were set in place before the current regime. They were anticipating that classified information would be utilized against anyone without them knowing it."

"C'mon … Who would use someone else's chromo, audio, and olfactosyncs as a lethal weapon?"

"You'll find out soon enough," he answers cryptically.

"Social security numbers, account numbers, passwords were wiped out because of so many security breaches in the past. There wasn't any other form of personal information left other than fingerprints, which, as we know, can be easily altered. That's why we're down to the basics, our senses."

"I think I get it now; there's no way to figure out how someone reacts or responds to certain things. For example, I …"

Josef gives me 'a look' and shakes his head. I guess it's time to move on to another subject, but how can I keep his attention during the rest of the ride?

"How about a game of chess?" I request.

Josef responds, "Feeling competitive, I see."

A chessboard appears on the Glåsse in front of us. The clock gives us five minutes each. After fourteen moves, neither of us has used more than a half minute on our clocks. Josef pauses briefly, stares at me with those eyes, and moves in a completely different direction than expected. He's playing much more aggressively than usual. The center of the board becomes a war zone, and I'm almost out of time. I completed my thirty-second move, and he still has over two minutes left.

"Times up!" He says, smiling big.

"Darn!" I exclaim.

Wonder if he beat me so badly because of what he's reading in that military manual.

He smiles that smile, "You played quite well, Jess, you're a great opponent and strategist."

"But I lost," I say, looking down.

"It's how you played, not whether you won or lost. I made it purposely tough on you." He admits.

"You did, why?"

Jazz's lovely pale pink sphere appears in the nick of time, allowing Josef to return to his military manual.

"Just spoke to Tomas, he has a friend in Dallas with some interesting tech data having to do with today's events. Would you be open to getting together with them later on?"

I respond, "You're so into 'everything Tomas,' I don't get it, but if it's important to you, it's important to me. I can do it at 7:30 pm."

What's wrong with me? I just used Josef's phrase. Have I lost every ounce of integrity and originality that I have to borrow everyone else's lines and ideas?

The pale sphere returns, "Tomas — 7:30 pm — yes. Friend tbd, c u later."

I turn to Josef and share. "A group of us are getting together at 7:30 tonight to review today's events. Would you be able to join us?" I ask, hoping he'll agree. "I'd appreciate your vision and impartiality."

Admittedly, I'd want him around because it'll force me to be more 'civilized' with Tomas.

"Sure, but we're going to need to include someone who knows a lot about security. From this point on, our communications would need to be private."

"Do you know someone who might be able to help us with that?" I ask eagerly.

"I might." He smiles mysteriously.

Just as I'm thinking of Jazz, her pink sphere drifts in. "Guess what? Josef is joining us tonight. Can we talk to Tomas' friend beforehand? Josef wants to know who he is and what qualifies him to talk about tech."

"I'll do my best. Have fun with your cute boyfriend."

Wonder if we should be referring to him as my boyfriend? By the way he treats me, he may just be my friend who happens to be a boy. It hurts just thinking about it.

We've reached our stop. It's exciting to be at Grand Central Station.

We agree to take a car to the WLC instead of walking. Our driver is a nonstop talker and only pauses when I interrupt by exclaiming, "Look at the tons of kids that are showing up!"

"Must be something exciting happening here for you guys today. Some sort of youth concert?"

Josef and I look at each other in disbelief and say nothing.

The driver seems oblivious, "To think this was the United Nations Building just a couple of months ago and now it's the World Leaders Conference Headquarters. You call it the WLC now, right?"

Josef responds, "Yes sir."

"Are you as sad as I am to see all the colorful flags gone? What's with these new ones, huh? I'm a veteran, and it would be hard to feel patriotic if I had to look at these gray and white rags flapping around in the wind."

"If you ask me, it's all a nightmare. The building used to be all windows and now it's a solid column of pure concrete with a few little peep holes. It gives me claustrophobia just looking at it." I say under my breath. Josef gives me a 'look'.

"Well kids, this is as close as I can get you to the entrance. Nice to meet some of our future leaders of the world, have fun!"

"Thank you, sir," Josef responds again.

As we walk towards the building, I turn to Josef, "What was that all about? Future leaders of the world? How could he be so unaware of what's going on here today?"

"Maybe it's not that he's unaware, he could be a spy. The last thing we need is to fall into an anti-patriotic conversation with a stranger. Especially someone from an unknown country on the way to the WLC."

"Wow, that didn't even occur to me, you are in military mode. I thought that his comments could imply that the brown haze didn't overtake everyone. Maybe adults didn't see or hear the announcement."

"That's very insightful, or it's a great conspiracy theory."

"It would sure explain why my parents were so quiet this morning. How could they not come upstairs when I was screaming my head off, and Jake was destroying his bedroom? Do you think they could have been controlled through their devices?"

"Interesting, you may be on to something. Right now, we need to be focused on today's event so we can figure out exactly why we're here. We are a good team, Jessica Stafford."

So glad he reconsidered the benefits of being here; I feel validated.

There are two men at the entrance wearing bulletproof vests and holding ginormous automatic rifles. The crowd parts in silence as we walk up to the gate. One of the guards gives Josef a dirty look.

"There are no seats left, kid; we've been instructed not to let anybody else in, especially military cadet types like you. Go back to where you came from."

Josef doesn't react; he looks straight ahead while I touch my device and show it to the unfriendly guard by the gate.

"Excuse me sir, you may be interested in seeing this. Here's our confirmation notice, our pictures, names, and seat numbers." The guard smirks, acts dismissive, and reluctantly opens the gate to let us in. Once we're inside the building, I say to Josef, "You sure kept your cool."

"No big deal, I wasn't about to fall for that childish move. He was trained to entrap and provoke incidents. Besides, if I fell for it, I'd be competing with you for notoriety. I'm not that competitive."

"Yeah, right." I punch him in the arm. Wow, his arm is as solid as a tree. We ride the escalator in silence to the top floor, where we see lots of agitated kids, scrambling and making sure they're in the right section. We walk towards our assigned entrance, Josef pulls the heavy doors wide open.

"Listen to that powerful roar coming from thousands of young people's voices, how exciting!" He remarks in awe.

"I don't feel that way at all," I say, feeling suddenly overwhelmed.

The sound is so powerful that it pushes my petite frame back like a strong gust of wind. Lights are dimmed, but we're still able to find our seats. We're at the very top, so our backs will be up against the concrete wall.

"Well, at least we know that nobody will be able to stab us in the back way up here." I joke when I'm nervous, and Josef ignores me. He's in hyper-vigilant military mode.

It's impossible to decipher what anyone is saying, but it's not necessary, their body language says it all. Some kids are sitting in silence with arms crossed, looking down, tapping their feet nervously, while others are standing in the aisles, gesturing and waving their arms, very upset.

"Josef, I'm feeling lightheaded and overwhelmed by the chaos."

"We can leave before they close the doors, it's now or never." As he offers an escape, I'm distracted by a couple of girls sitting to my left. One is sobbing while the other is trying to comfort her. I recognize the older of the two.

"Excuse me, is everything alright? Hi, I'm Jessica Stafford." I say, extending my hand.

She stares and replies, "I know exactly who you are."

Did I just mess up? I shouldn't have brought attention to myself. What if she asks for an autograph? What if the press locates me?

"You know Jasmin Ross, right?" She asks.

"Yes, I do know her."

I'm so incredibly full of myself, she recognizes me not as the unwilling media sensation, but as a ninth-grader in Eastchester High School.

"I've seen you at her house. We live on the next block over. I'm Becca, and this is my sister Sammie."

"Small world, Jazz's house, right, sure." I try to save face in case my conceit came through loud and clear. Sure hope she can't read minds. I hope she hasn't seen my hopeless watercolor attempts either.

Josef leans over just at the right moment. He smiles gently at both girls and says, "Junior Cadet Josef Tallon-Saldane at your service, ladies."

He reaches in front of me to shake hands with each of the girls. He's such a gentleman, he distracted them and made them feel special — reason #498 as to why I like him.

"May I help you with something?" He asks the crying Sammie. She can barely look at him, let alone speak.

"I, um, I'm um ..."

"Take a deep breath; it really helps us when we're upset." He says softly. She inhales, making her little cheeks blow up like small red balloons that are about to pop. It would be so cute if only she weren't so upset.

"I'm really scared," she says as she exhales and starts sobbing again. She takes another big gulp of air and turns even redder.

She's calm enough to speak. "Becca said I had to come and see this mean horrible man in person, I hate him, and I didn't want to; he gives me bad dreams. She said it's okay to be scared and that we all have to learn to face our fears, so why not start today." She bursts out in tears and so does her sister.

I'm trying to keep it together, but inside, I feel just like them.

"Becca, how old are you?" Josef asks.

"Going to be thirteen next week." She replies, sniffling.

"You know what, Sammie, you have a very smart big sister and she's looking out for you."

Both girls are staring at him, holding on to every word.

"Do you want to know a secret?" He asks.

They nod wide-eyed.

"Jess and I are also scared, but we decided to come down and see it all for ourselves. Once we know what to expect, we can make plans. Jess, shall we invite them to be on our team?"

"Sure." I nod, pretending to know what he's talking about.

"We're looking for qualified imaginarians."

"Why?" Becca asks.

"Because every time The World Chancellor says something upsetting, we need people to visualize the exact opposite that will start creating our new reality."

"I don't know what that means." Sammie looks confused.

"What's your favorite shape?" Josef asks her.

"I looove circles." She says, smiling for the first time.

"So if today he declares that all circles are going away, your job is to start imagining lots and lots of circles."

"Purple ones and pink ones?"

Josef nods, smiling big, "You got it!"

"So, ladies, are you in?"

"We'll try," Becca responds, looking a bit puzzled.

Sammie clings to her arm, saying, "I love circles, but I'm still scared."

I'm blown away by how he handled their fears. I turn my back to the girls and mouth, "Thank you, you're wonderful." A heavy tear rolls down my face.

Becca reaches over to hug her sister and not being my style at all; I join in for a group hug. The other kids around us start doing the same thing. Our emotions are spontaneous and natural. It feels good 'to feel.'

I break away and lean over towards Josef.

"Children consoling children, beautifully tragic, isn't it?" I share.

"It's a matter of survival. I had to come up with ways of making it through tough times when Stefan and I ..." He whispers teary-eyed.

Lights come up full blast, the auditorium quiets down, and the projection on the wall shows it's exactly 3:00 PM.

"Oh joy," I whisper over to Josef.

"Shh ... shh ..." Comes from somewhere close by.

There are two small doors on either side of the stage's raised platform. They open simultaneously, and from our vantage point, it seems as if two giant gray snakes slither out, one from each opening. My ocular implants adjust, and I realize they're not snakes at all; they're adults walking very close to one another. They're all wearing identical clothing in that same sickly pasty gray. The jumpsuits and the skull caps that conceal their hair and ears make it impossible to tell a man from a woman. How disturbing, I feel nauseous. The snake-like formations break apart, and each 'being' takes its place around an immense crescent-shaped table, cloaked in heavy black fabric.

What happened to all these people? They're not even blinking; they're just looking straight ahead.

"Our world will never be the same again," I whisper.

Josef tilts his head towards me without losing focus.

"Shh ... shh ..."

The Chancellor makes his entrance by rising center stage on an ascending platform. His image is enlarged on the screen behind him for all to see. He's appropriately attired in doomsday black and holding what looks like a royal scepter in his right hand. Talk about delusional.

His *ensemble* is absolutely ridiculous looking. Jazz will be so proud that I'm using her favorite French fashionista term. Clearly no one has told him that his 'look' fails to conceal his considerable girth and minuscule height. Jazz would do wonders for him as his image consultant. He's wearing a velvet jacket with padded shoulders and wide satin lapels. His shirt has a much too tight priest-like collar. The slacks are way too long and bunch up on his shoes which are typically worn by male *flamenco* dancers. Why does he wear gloves all the time? If he were my client I'd tell him that his high heels in no way make up for his low moral standards. I've heard adults say that his slick black patent leather looking hair and long sideburns make him look like an Elvis Impersonator. Who is Elvis anyway, and why are people always impersonating him?

Once the 'elevated' performance ends, he approaches a gaudy red leather throne centered at the crescent table. His assistant's left sleeve has a black band around the forearm. His job is to make sure his leader is safely seated. The scepter is leaning against the chair's right arm. The assistant then hands him a stack of documents.

The house lights go down. A theatrical spotlight washes over him, casting an eerie shadow on his face. I keep looking at the snakelings, trying to recognize them. Are these the same world leaders who walked in this morning, defiant and ready to fight for our rights? How has he managed, within hours, to strip them of their identity, their voice, and their independence? This is looking more and more diabolical by the minute.

My skin is starting to itch and burn.

Is this what Josef was referring to when someone accesses hue. r.u. quotients? How could he know about this in advance?

A faceless voice fills the auditorium.

"Members of the audience, if you choose to remain for the entire duration of the assembly, The World Chancellor demands proper decorum. Speaking and shouting are absolutely forbidden. Standing or walking around will not be tolerated. Breaking these rules will result in severe punishment."

Nothing like starting an event by being threatened. I turn to Josef, and he's looking straight ahead. The Chancellor begins speaking with his inimitable dissonant voice, "Members of the council, you have had sufficient time to review the proposition regarding the elimination of all future functions of micro and nano devices implanted in subhumans under eighteen years of age."

The Chancellor looks to the left and the right.

"Are there any questions before we proceed to the vote?"

A 'being' on the panel turns towards him, shyly raising a hand.

The request is ignored.

"Excellent! No questions, let's proceed."

Roars, screams, and booing erupt from the audience.

He reaches for his scepter and uses it on the stage floor like a giant gavel, "Silence, I say, silence!"

He waves over the attendant and whispers into his cap. The attendant walks over to the snakeling, who obviously doesn't understand the meaning of a rhetorical question. It's lifted, seat and all, and is promptly removed from the stage. In less than thirty seconds, the attendant returns as if nothing has happened and takes his place next to The Chancellor. His shirt sleeve now has a red band below the original black.

"What is that all about?" I whisper. Josef shakes his head as he's looking intently at the stage.

The Ogre exclaims. "Let's proceed with the vote!"

There are rumblings and grumblings in the auditorium.

The giant gavel is used again as a reminder not to speak.

The screen behind him shows a pale gray silhouette of the world. Small black marks begin dotting each country, covering the maps almost completely. A few reds and yellows pop up. The Chancellor is alerted by the assistant to turn around and look.

He growls, "I am absolutely disgusted and horrified!

Despite the evidence, there are still questions and disagreements about the fate of The Hybrids? I demanded a unanimous vote — and that's what we shall have. Your lack of moral standards as leaders is highly disappointing. You have betrayed me ... and your fellow countrymen!"

He pauses and barks, "Gentlemen, with the authority vested in me, I formally declare we have triumphed over The Hybrids with a unanimous vote. We can now disempower subhumans everywhere!"

Everyone, except for Josef, stomps our feet in protest. A group yells out, "Outrageous, not unanimous! Yellows and reds are people! Outrageous, not unanimous! Yellows and reds are people!"

A group of armed guards rushes over to grab the dissenters who spoke out. I'm too upset to think what's going to happen to them now. If I could look at my Intellitela, it would be flaming screaming red. I'm in volcanic mode, about to explode. Becca and Sammie are sobbing.

"The statute to deactivate the implants goes into effect at once!" The Chancellor proclaims. His impassioned gaveling pierces through the raised platform's floor.

The giant screen shows a statement in pale gray letters against a black background:

> The WLC concludes this session
> proclaiming a unanimous vote!
> Penalties for not abiding by the regulations
> set forth on this day of ____ will be enforced
> to the full extent of the law
> effective as of ____ AM/PM EST

Josef tilts his head discretely towards the screen to point out the glaring *faux pas*. The date and time were left blank, so no matter what, The Ogre was going to declare victory.

I lean towards Josef, whispering, "What an injustice, what a total fraud. Whoever forgot to fill in today's date is going to be severely punished."

"Shhh … shhh …"

A scream is heard close to the stage. A Security Cluster scurries in again and huddles around someone who's fainted on the floor. A large man scoops her up by the waist like a rag doll and walks away. The whole auditorium seems to gasp.

The faceless voice announces, "Until his excellency, The World Chancellor and the distinguished panel empty the stage; you may not exit, speak or shout out."

"Not unless you happen to be him or you happen to faint," I whisper.

"Shhh … shhh …"

I stomp my foot in frustration, but what I actually need is to pull on my hair or scream or something for immediate relief.

His Ogerness steps down from his bloody throne, refusing help.

Josef leans over, whispering, "Trouble in Paradise."

We watch the last of the beings slither out of sight as the side doors close behind them and the house lights go up. There are no words to explain what everyone looks like and what the auditorium feels like. I have to contain my emotions because I'm fully visible and because I need to make sure the young sisters are alright.

The four of us make it out as a group all the way down to the lobby. I loop my right arm through Josef's left, which gives me strength. My other arm goes around Sammie's delicate trembling shoulder. I look up at Josef, my handsome cadet's eyes are filled with tears.

"It was nice to meet you, and thank you," Becca says as she takes her sister's hand and brings her towards herself. We spill out onto the street with the stunned masses.

I'm completely spent, so my arms fall to my sides. Josef grabs my right hand as we weave our way through the crowds. We start running.

"Josef, where are we going?"

His index finger covers his mouth.

After a few blocks, I implore, "Stop Josef, please stop!"

We are zipping past buildings and shops on 42nd. I really wish we could stop for a second. We slow down enough for me to say, "My legs aren't long enough to keep up with your Olympic pace." He points at a bench for us to sit on about a block from The Chrysler Building. He needs to catch his breath too.

"What were we running from?" I ask panting.

"We had to get out of the security radius to speak freely. For a little girl, you kept up pretty well."

"I'm considered petite, don't ever call me little again. Understood?"

"Yes, ma'am!" He salutes, making an extra serious face.

"So, how do you think this is going to play out? Are our own parents expected to turn us into the authorities? How are we going to function without technology?"

"I don't know, nobody knows, exactly."

"Then, I'm going to need the demographics for our age group."

"What for?" He asks.

"His Ogerness is in for a big surprise. The Hybrids are about to become 'his' worst nightmare."

"Did you go into strategic mode before my very eyes? Now that's the Jess I know and love!"

"What did you just say?" I ask, wanting to hear it again.

He smiles his smile.

My heart rate shot up. How can I hide that I'm shaking?

"Wow, it's colder than I thought, even with all the running. Crazy, I'm still shaking," I say.

He blushes and I break the silence by saying. "I do my best thinking when I'm walking, not running. I need to sort out some stuff for tonight. Okay if we walk back to Grand Central?"

"Yeah, sure, thank you for including me in your plans." He says, smiling. "I have some steam to blow off myself. I'm worried, I haven't had a chance to talk to my brother yet. I need to get his feedback on how this is playing out at the academy."

"Is it safe to do that? What if that network is monitored?"

"It might be the other way around; the school may be monitoring what's going on, on the outside. They built the barracks less than a year ago with state-of-the-art technology. Woodland Military School may appear to be your typical high school, but it was designed to function as a fully-equipped military base in case of a national emergency."

I stare at him as he's speaking but my thoughts are already shifting towards getting a team together to combat The Evil One.

"I have a question for you." I ask.

"Another one? I hope it isn't controversial." He kids.

"Would you say you're a military genius?"

"Jess, just because I play a good game of chess ..."

I interrupt, "No, seriously, what you're reading is so advanced."

"I've always liked military strategy, that's what got me into The Academy. Reading this advanced manual will get me into The Special Forces Division."

"Impressive!" I say, pretending to know what that means.

"May I ask you a hypothetical question?"

He stares and frowns. "I thought you were supposed to be walking and thinking, not walking and asking!"

"I was thinking and now I'm asking." I snap.

"Okay ... what is it?"

"Let's say you had access to schematics of manufacturing plants and warehouses that were filled with weapons."

He looks perplexed, "What are you talking about?"

"Could you devise a plan for their removal?"

"Where are these hypothetical weapons housed, and what do you mean by removing them?"

"Hypothetically, they could be in Russia or China or even India. Who knows. Removing meaning eliminating them from the face of the planet." I wince.

"Why are you asking me such an outlandish question?"

"I'm gauging your capabilities for my hypothetical plan. Do you think your professors would assist you with something like this, Junior Cadet Josef Tallon-Saldane?"

"They would question my motives, and they'd be watching me very closely. The plan is too realistic."

"Hmm ..."

Tomas' colorless sphere glides in on my device.

"Hey Tomas, I'm here with Josef, we just left the WLC."

"Tomas, hey, Josef here. Is it okay to connect in a few?"

"Umm ... yeah ... guess so." Tomas sounds confused.

"That was rather territorial of you, taking over my communication with Tomas like that." I state.

"I had to make a quick decision. We can't speak to him anymore without the proper security."

"Oh, you're right."

We get to the station and rush to an empty table to activate the Glåsse.

Tomas is waiting impatiently and asks, "Hey, Josef, why are you there with Jess, I thought you were supposed to be in military school?"

"My job today was to make sure Jess was escorted safely to the WLC."

There's a long silence … Oh no, I wonder if Tomas is weirded out already.

"Stand by. Do you see this?" Tomas asks.

The window on the Glåsse flickers a couple of times and then turns white. Then we see an image of an ancient stone bridge supported by two arches.

"Touch what you see," Tomas instructs.

We each choose an arch and place our thumbs inside the curvatures.

The image dissolves and a very serious Tomas appears.

"We've done what you asked," Josef states.

Below the image, text appears, 'Access the local news on the regular network and mute.'

"Okay, we're now inside a secure network and we're free to speak. Only a few of us are authorized to use it." Tomas clarifies.

"Tomas, you have thought of everything, this is quite impressive," I say.

"I didn't think of asking you for a secure connection, thanks Tomas." Josef inserts.

"I have friends that designed this. I can't take credit for it."

"Can we meet with your friends before 7:30 tonight?" I inquire.

"No, not possible, but they'll be there at 7:30 pm."

I nod and after a short awkward silence, Tomas responds, "Later."

His image fades away.

"This is a whole other side of Tomas I've never seen before; he's unrecognizably focused and professional."

"I keep telling you Jess, he's a good guy, a bit intense, that's all. You can relate, can't you?" Josef asks.

"Jazz feels the same way about him as you do. She can see beyond his 'oddities.' In all fairness, I may be intense, but I'm not as odd as he is. Am I?"

Josef creates a distraction and changes the subject.

"Look over there, an energy drink stand. I need something fresh and natural; my treat."

Glad he's offering to pay but not glad when I see who's working there. It's none other than, Ms. Everything I'm Not. She's tall, cute with silky blond hair and big green eyes. If she blinks quickly one more time, she's going to start a *tsunami.* How dare she flirt so openly with him in front of me. Look at him, he's clueless, and he's falling right into it. Grrr …

She smiles and says, "Josef, hope y'all enjoy your drinks? It's so nice of you to bring your little 'sistah' along 'fo' the day. No sitters available?"

"What did you just say?" I ask indignantly.

She looks at me for a split second and refocuses on Josef, who says absolutely nothing. I'm so angry right now. I have to make a gargantuan effort to hold my tongue. We walk away, sipping in silence as I desperately try to find something emerald green to use for self-balancing.

"I can't get through to Stefan," Josef says, sounding rather upset.

As were walking by a vacant cafe, I suggest, "Must be that the system is overloaded. Try using the Glåsse on this table instead." We sit next to each other.

I clarify, "Bet it's crashing because of the event at The WLC. This happened once before during Sahrit's first international concert."

"How did you get so smart, Ms. Stafford?"

"Oh ... I don't know; maybe it runs in the family; after all, I am your little sister." I say, jabbing him in the ribs with my elbow.

"Ouch! What are you talking about?"

"That blond Southern belle at the juice stand referred to me as your little sister, needing babysitting. You didn't correct her. I'm feeling insulted."

"She said that? How ridiculous, we don't even look anything alike."

He chuckles.

I frown at him.

"Jess, I'm a guy, remember? I didn't hear any of it. I was preoccupied with more important things, like Stefan and the future of the world."

I'm so embarrassed; I could just dissolve on the floor.

I hear Jazz coming through faintly. "Hey, can you hear me? I can only use sound, no image capability. The system's overloaded, just like what happened at Sahrit's first international concert."

"Wow, that's exactly what I told Josef. You'll never guess who was sitting next to me at the WLC?"

"Becca and Sammie, perhaps?" She says with a British accent.

"Yeah — Wait, you already knew?"

"I knew they were going, so I maneuvered their seating. It's a family tradition, I'll tell you about that sometime. I had a feeling the girls needed to hear whatever you two had to say."

"Jazz Ross, you're always looking out for everyone else. Credit where credit is due, it was Josef who made a difference in their lives. He's great with kids."

"So I hear from Stefan."

Butterfly-like flutters start on my right cheek and then on the left, signaling I was kind and considerate of others. Yes!

"What was it like being in the same space as The World Dictator?" She asks.

"Even so far up in the stands, you could feel the thickness of his evil. It wasn't brown but gray, pasty, sickly. To get over it, we're having energy fruit drinks right now."

"Nothing like getting something fresh and natural to offset the rotten and artificial." Jazz giggles and then changes her tone. "Jess, whatever you say to me from this point on, is water under the bridge. Alright?"

That lets us know we're speaking in the secure network now.

"Got it. Guess what? Josef will join us at 7:30 tonight."

"Now that I can speak freely … You're getting the military involved? What are you planning to do?" Jazz sounds concerned.

"I'm not quite sure yet, but what I do know is that the junior cadets we know and trust are highly qualified. This is all going to come down to one thing and one thing only — strategy."

"In the meantime, Jazz, my dearest friend of friends and trusted personal assistant *extraordinaire*, can you do something for me before tonight's meeting?" I request sweetly.

"Umm … It all depends …" She responds.

"I need some demographics; here are the details."

There's a pause, and then she laughs her wonderful laugh.

"Thank you, I needed a good laugh today."

"What do you mean?" I wonder.

"You're serious? … You really think I can do all this by tonight? No way, and even if I could, I wouldn't because I have plans with Stefan. He has partial leave today and wants to be with *moi*."

"I can be such a demanding jerk sometimes. Can't I?" Josef looks up and smiles.

"Jazz, you're always the giver and I'm the ultimate taker in our relationship. That's twice in one day I've upset you." Josef looks up, but this time, he frowns.

"Tell me the truth. Have I always been so bossy?" I ask reluctantly.

"Umm … well, to be honest, yes, you have, but I've always sensed you had a mission in life. Perhaps this is the moment for which you were created." Jazz recites poetically.

"You're like Queen Esther."

"Really? Who is she?"

I'm so flattered she sees me as royalty.

"She was a highly courageous woman, instrumental in changing the world in her day. Look her up sometime — soon!"

"I will, but one more thing before you go."

"You're relentless, aren't you?" Jazz says.

Josef chuckles as I bat my eyelashes at him.

"Jazz, I want you to copilot this project with me. I also want you to come up with the theme song for our initiative."

"Ommm ...." By the sound of her breathing, I know she's closed her eyes and gone into a deep meditation.

Josef looks at me with a question on his face.

Jazz resurfaces less than a minute later with the perfect answer.

"Flower Power, Sahrit Bana's latest hit."

fears

On the way back home from the station, I decide it's time to get to the bottom of why my brother and I have such volatile personalities. My parents are pretty even-tempered and world-famous for avoiding conflict and controversy at all costs. There must be more to Mom, there's no way she could've always been so peaceful and optimistic, but that's the only way I've ever known her to be.

I may look like a mini version of her, but our personalities are very different. She loves staying at home, cooking, baking, and gardening. My Dad calls her his Domestic Goddess. My use of eucalyptus and lavender comes from her. She got into selling natural products, like herbs and scents and stuff, when she found out that could help me calm down, because of my sensory overload issues. None of her potions seems to work for Jake, but only because he won't give it a try. He says that's girl stuff. Jake disputes everything that comes his way, even if it's for his own good.

Jake looks like a rougher burlier version of Dad but that's all they seem to have in common. My brother would never be considered a well read deep thinker. Jake and I are most definitely not adopted like Jazz and her sweet brother Sy. We're like our parents, just modified versions.

I so hope Mom and Dad have a secret past; it would make them much more interesting. I guess I'm spoiled by having such a close relationship with Jazz's parents. They're intriguing and very accomplished.

Just as I walk in the front door, a dark green sphere floats in on my device, "Jess, want to chat about today's events?"

Hmm … Interesting coming from Dad.

"When?"

"Come in 10 minutes, I'll be up for a break then."

I decide to listen to music for a while to decompress. My thoughts drift towards gratitude, and that leads me to appreciate the Intellitela. Where would I be without a system that anticipates my needs or calls me out on my misdeeds? It lets me know what I'm feeling before I know it myself. If I'm not going in the right direction, a 'Thought Interrupter' bleeps and sends me messages on the screen, or I may get a body sensation. Wind chimes are my auditory reward, indicating I've understood and internalized information. The screen turns different colors, according to what's brewing inside of me. Orangey red is a warning and red is big trouble. The hue.r.u's are different for everyone. We can program some codes, but others have to be done at The Recalibration Center. Wonder what will be taking place at the Centers if our nanotechnology is being disabled. My alarm indicates it's time to meet with Dad. I gallop downstairs to the rhythm of the music in my head.

Before I even knock on the door, he says, "Come in." He swivels around slowly, wearing his rarely seen smile.

"I heard your eagerness playing out on the stairs. I'm flattered you accepted my invitation."

Dad's office faces the back yard, so even if his window is small, he has a really nice view. Mom made sure of it; she created a little oasis with a water feature and everything. When the weather is nice, he keeps his window open. It makes up for the chaos inside. His tiny room used to be the mud room. It's filled with all kinds of boxes holding who knows what. Guess there's no room for them in the closet or the file cabinet. Dad used to go to an actual office and maybe he's never adjusted to the reality of his permanency of working at home.

"Your timing was excellent, Dad; I've got serious existential problems that need serious answers."

He fidgets in his creaky office chair. "Shouldn't you be talking to your mom about this kind of thing?"

"This isn't girl stuff, Dad," I say impatiently. "You know Mom. She gets overly emotional about everything. I need practical straight up solutions."

"In that case, you're in the right place, ma'am." He replies.

He leans back and points at the green chair next to him. I clear my throat and blurt out, "After much analysis, I've determined that I'm an insolent, impatient, insecure controlling fixer perfectionist with a bad temper. So during these times of uncertainty and impending doom, I'm finding it very hard to live with myself."

"That's quite an opening statement, tell me more, but this time, break it down for me."

Typical me, I'm already put out by his request. I have this ridiculous notion that Dad can decode everything I say or think without further explanation.

"Alright … I'm totally frustrated and feel powerless with what I see on my platform, Liberty World. Is that better?" I say with escalating annoyance.

"Tone it down, young lady." He instructs.

"Sorry, Dad. See what I mean about my temper?"

He smiles and nods, motioning me to continue.

"My platform is being bombarded with messages from all over the world from kids my age and younger. Their feelings are ranging from scared to absolutely petrified, and you know how bad I am with feeling related matters."

Dad looks at me, intently. "They're not your strongest talent, but you have many others."

"Even seeing it that way, these kids still want guidance on how to process what they're feeling and thinking. It's only going to get worse after today's announcements at the WLC. They're going to expect immediate answers on what's going to happen right after our nano implants are disabled. As if I knew. They're going to expect solutions on how to handle life without the technology we're all accustomed to."

Dad asks, "Are they indicating in any way that they expect immediate solutions coming specifically from you? I want you to think before you answer."

"Well ... no, not exactly, but if they're contacting me, isn't it implied?"

"Not necessarily, you've offered them a safe environment in which to express their feelings, so they're expressing."

"Oh great — then I've created a huge problem for myself by offering this forum. The way I process information, even if they don't say it, I feel a sense of urgency to solve all their problems. Instead of feeling gratified and flattered, I feel a deep sense of responsibility and horrible pressure that's eating me up inside."

"Oh, Jessy." He says, leaning forward, opening his hands so they can cradle mine. I pull back, rejecting the offer as if it could hurt me. I just keep venting.

"Dad, I know exactly what you're going to tell me. You are going to say that the right thing to do is to step up to the plate, take responsibility for my actions, and somehow fulfill people's expectations. Right?"

"No, not necessarily. If you were so sure of what I was going to say, why did you accept my invitation?"

The throbbing in my wrists means that I'm feeling embarrassed on top of the frustration brewing inside. I hate the wrist thing; it's so out of character for me.

"You and Mom and everybody have such high expectations of me as a superhuman. I feel the pressure of always having to be perfectly perfect all the time. What choice do I have?" My tone is getting really bad.

Dad shifts from active listener to Sensory Coach.

"Jess, do your emerald green thing, I'm right here."

I take a deep breath and close my eyes. Images come of happy times when Dad and I would check on the growth patterns and color changes of leaves. I was fascinated by the process and the patterns and how they went from bright green to a lush deep emerald. I can almost hear the rustling sounds of the wind blowing through the trees. I feel warm tears roll down my cheeks. I exhale. I open my eyes and see Dad's eyes gleaming with tears.

"Thanks for helping avert a volcanic incident, Coach."

"I experienced your memory, honey, it was beautiful. Let's get back to decoding what you said earlier."

"I know I'm really bright and really good at some things, but I also realize that's not enough to make everyone else happy. It's sure not making me happy. I have to accept that I'm just a kid, not a mini adult with an arsenal filled with 40 years of life experiences. This is all very scary and confusing. I have no idea how to feel, other than scared. What can I do about it?" I say, crying.

"Right now, you just need time to figure things out like everyone else." Dad smiles lovingly.

"It's hard to admit, but my arrogance and illusionary superhero persona have gotten me in trouble, as usual."

He leans towards me once again, and this time I accept his cradling invitation; my hands are shaking.

"Jess, listen to me very carefully. I don't want you to get discouraged by scary monologues filled with darkness. They're designed to distract everyone by creating fear and insecurity."

"To distract us from what?" I ask.

"We don't know what's being hidden, but ..."

"But what, Dad?"

"The toughest part for you will be to learn how to cope with your vulnerability. Last time I checked, it's not a crime to feel your feelings. In fact, it's a strength, especially in an effective leader."

"You mean like The Illustrious Chancellor?" I ask tongue in cheek.

He skips over my comment. "You're becoming a very good leader Jess, but as a fourteen-year-old, you need to see what's behind that tough warrior exterior ..."

"That's very scary, dealing with emotions and stuff."

He looks annoyed at me because I've picked up his bad habit of interrupting conversations.

"If I may continue ... you have to tap into your emotions because you'll discover that you share all the same fears and insecurities your friends have. Start acknowledging your feelings, all of them, good and bad. Is there stuff inside of you, and you don't know where it's coming from? The answer is yes. It's part of who you are and who you will be for the foreseeable future."

"I'm not sure I understand."

He looks out the window, takes a deep breath, and looks back at me.

"Part of the implant process, shall we say, altered children's memory about how they dealt with certain experiences. The feelings are there but not the story behind it."

"Does this have anything to do with our bad tempers?"

Dad ignores the comment and continues. "While I was on the advisory board, I lost an important battle that affected every child on the planet. My position was that what we learn until the age of six is invaluable. Unfortunately, my opinion was overturned by the implant manufacturers and their investors. They failed to find the relevance of that fact since the nano implants promised to teach children how to recognize emotional signals. They claimed that the past didn't matter because you'd all be starting over anyway."

"The nano implant manufacturers and all the investors got to decide what would happen to our childhood memories? That's monstrous!" I yell jumping up from my chair. "They kidnapped a part of me and they don't think it's even worth asking for a ransom. Are my memories stored anywhere?"

Dad looks at the boxes on the floor longingly and his chin quivers.

"Dad, are our memories stored in all these boxes?" I ask with a glimmer of hope.

"I managed to save as much as I could, but unfortunately, the printouts are all encrypted data. I've never had the heart to get rid of any of it."

"Can you decode it?" I exclaim.

"So very sorry, Jessy, I've really tried. Without the memories or the nanos, you're going to have to start from a new beginning. You'll be like a baby learning how to walk and talk for the first time. You'll get up and fall and try again until you figure it out. It's going to be frustrating, but your mom and I are here to support you and your brother in every way possible. If it makes you feel any better, adults also have existential crises and don't always figure things out."

"So what you're saying is that I better research how people dealt with feelings before nano implants existed?"

"Yes, you need to. Adults' memories weren't removed or altered, so ask us whenever you need to."

"How can I possibly move forward knowing that our memories were removed and destroyed."

"I wish I had a sensible answer for you, but I don't. I'd like to say that the rage you and Jake feel, comes from sensing that a part of you is missing. There may be some truth to that and the rest may be in these boxes."

"Can you believe that just today, I decided to discover the source of our anger, and now I find out it's in a box?" I snap back with frustration.

"Even though Jake and I are total opposites, we share you as parents and we both experience the same rage. I need to get to the bottom of this somehow."

Dad seems to tense up.

"Dad, do you have time for more questions?"

He nods though he looks a bit nervous.

"We were told that the implants were going to be disabled immediately. Have they or haven't they? I haven't been feeling 100% today."

"Can you expand on that?" Dad requests.

"Well, for example, I noticed that I've been using some of my friends' ideas and expressions as if they were mine. I've hurt Jazz's and Josef's feelings several times today, beyond the norm, and I didn't realize it till after the fact."

"If you had never gotten implants, I'd say that you and your friends are really in tune with each other and that you pick up on each other's vibe. As for hurting feelings, that's an unavoidable consequence of being a teenager."

"Well, that's something to look forward to," I say sarcastically.

Dad leans back in his chair again and looks into the distance. "Listen to me carefully and do not share this with anyone. Understood?"

"Yes sir, you have my word."

"Those who prepared the information for the WLC's announcement aren't as knowledgeable as they claim to be. They don't realize that as long as the technology remains inside the body, it contains a certain percentage of reserve."

"Really? How long do we have left?" I ask urgently.

"It will dwindle slowly until they are fully disabled. You will have a maximum of seven to ten days, depending on each kid's personality and what programs they access."

"I have to confess something." I pause and take a deep breath. "I've been resentful about your participation in the development of the micro and nano implants. I thought you were the enemy. Now I'm grateful that you're in the know."

"Sweetheart, I could never turn against you. My life's purpose has always been and always will be to enhance your life."

"Thanks, Daddy." I start crying, wishing I was young enough to still sit on his lap.

"How could I have ever imagined you as a villain? I do need to go back to something, though." I wince.

"Okay, but let's make it quick."

"Do you think that what's in the boxes has a connection to us having bad tempers?"

"That's not something I'm prepared to discuss right now."

"Okay, but some other time then?" I request.

"Maybe."

"I'm glad you get me, cuz I don't get myself most of the time."

"Welcome to this side of the genetic pool. You're a regular teen, Princessa. Now, let's speak about what I wanted to talk about. Okay?"

I nod, Dad continues, "Your Mom and I are still dealing with the consequences of your brother's involvement in the riots in Manhattan last December. We need to be reassured that you'll be responsible and won't get into any kind of trouble."

I respond, "I'm furious at all the protesters, one of which shall remain nameless. They messed things up for all of us by creating so much fear. Now we're paying the consequences by having our implants disabled. I can only promise to be responsible for the next two years. Research shows that the stupid gene kicks in when we turn sixteen."

Dad reaches for my hand, smiling at my witty comment.

We both feel better, and I give him a bear hug from behind. Mom has been working in the den. She heard the entire conversation. I walk over and kiss her on the cheek.

"Thank you, sweetie, we love you both, no matter what, with or without implants." She says lovingly.

"Guess it hasn't been exactly easy to love your little apples lately, huh?"

Mom looks down and smiles.

I run upstairs to my room. The Intellitela has set up the ambiance perfectly knowing what I need after my talk with Dad. The lighting is just so, and the spheres are gliding rhythmically to the most wonderful music. The delicate scent of lavender helps me relax. I gather up my industrial quantities of hair into a giant bun, prop up every one of my pillows against the headboard and scoot all the way back.

Ahh ... perfect. Okay, I'm ready to give tonight's meeting some thought. Tomas drives me up the wall and out the window, but in all fairness, he does have lots to offer. For us to have a successful collaboration, I need to make an effort to decipher why he annoys me to no end.

Bleep!

'Patience Is A Virtue' appears in emerald green letters on the upper right corner of the wall.

Bleep!

Carl Jung — The Shadow Self. Useful to understand conflicting feelings. Read more here.

That's intriguing. I'm saving that for later, much later ...

Enough of this heavy thinking, I'm drained, time for some healthy escapism.

The Intellitela starts listing options of what's available.

No ... boring ... not today ... ridiculous ... never ... forget that ... Perfect!

Today's new segment of 'Show Me Your True Colours' with Maarlee McGee is coming up in a few minutes.

I close my eyes; Maarlee's image comes to me. She's an intelligent, enthusiastic, glossy raven haired exotic looking girl with perfect pearly white teeth, who wears the greatest outfits, ever. She's calm all the time and has tons of confidence; nothing ever seems to rattle her. She has her whole act together. If I didn't like her so much, I'd really resent her.

Bleep!

My eyes open and see that the spheres on the Glåsse freeze in place, and the colors fade out. I can't help but smile; this entity has 'the virtual guts' to call me out on my stuff. I hurt Jazz earlier today and she didn't even hear me say the whole thing. I need to stop resenting my friends.

Thought Replacement – Say — 'I like her so much or I admire her so much, I'm going to learn by example or I'm going to emulate quality (X).'

Wind Chimes …

Dad said I have to be in touch with myself and face my feelings. The truth is, I believe that Maarlee and Jazz represent everything I'm not.

Bleep!

Look up Jealousy and Envy.

I'll do that later … much, much later.

Bleep!

Read more about Maarlee McGee.

'Show is currently the top teen feed in the world, fun format, elements of surprise, content always fresh, uplifting, inspiring, eye-opening. Host interviews people of all ages anywhere her guests feel inspired to open up. Dens, supermarkets, cafes, and even warehouses make for great venues. She never divulges where she is nor what she'll be discussing from week to week. Host is humble about her talents and doesn't bring attention to herself. She is generous with compliments and feelings.'

If only I could …

Bleep!

Okay, I get it, the message is as subtle as a locomotive.

Wind Chimes …

A few months ago, I became a financial supporter of her show. One of the benefits is having access to ten minutes of pre and post-show snippets.

Here we go …

Play …

The pre-show is starting … love this part.

Maarlee is reviewing questions, checking her beautiful hair and great outfit while she's making sure that today's show goes as planned and the guest feels welcome. Even if it's the pre-show, we can't see who's on. Production is on top of all the details; the show is seamless.

"Good Morning, we'll be on shortly. I'm so thrilled you agreed to join us today." Maarlee says to her guest.

We can't hear the response … hate this part.

Maarlee continues cheerfully, "I look forward to hearing about …"

The producer interrupts.

"Maar … 5, 4, 3, 2 … we are on the air…!"

"Hi everyone! Welcome, welcome! Glad you're here to Show Me Your True Colours. I'm Maarlee

McGee, streaming live from … somewhere on planet Earth …!" She says joyfully.

"I'm very excited to introduce my personal hero and role model, the very colorful and charming Ms. Zivah Zahav."

As Maarlee looks away from the camera, she faces the monitor. Her ocular nano implants are programmed so viewers can see what she sees, but only when she wants us to. She's modified her ocular implants to suit the show's purposes. Hardly nefarious, Mr. Chancellor. There are thousands upon thousands of comments from fans pouring in already and the interview hasn't even started. People love this guest. Where have I been, I've never heard of this person before? We still don't see who she's speaking to; we just see Maar from the camera's vantage point.

"Ms. Zahav, first things first, you're dressed in the most luscious looking garment. Please tell us more about it for all our fashionistas out there."

We now see a woman around my parent's age, mid to late thirties. I'm drawn to her glowing smile and her crown of oodles and poodles of auburn curly hair. Wow, talk about having a presence!

"You're such a dear to have me on, Maarlee. I'm thrilled you like what I'm wearing. May I ask you a question?"

"You want to ask me a question? Of course, Ms. Zahav."

"When you first meet a person, whether you speak to them or not, are you more aware of their physicality or their vibe?" She asks with a polished British accent.

"Does this have something to do with the idea that we are what we wear?" Maarlee inquires.

"Quite so. Some of us think we are expressing our essence by what we wear on the surface, but what we express comes from a much deeper place."

"Please say more about that, it's fascinating."

"Maybe some of us are afraid to express how we feel in words but can do it with our clothing and our accessories. Others, very consciously, think they can block their feelings to stay safe, but regardless, they're still emitting clues. Then there are people like myself who choose to be fully self-expressed through as many sensory outlets as possible."

The guest laughs out loud freely.

"I just love what you're saying!" Maarlee gushes, putting her hands to her heart.

Ms. Zahav continues, "I'm of the belief that each one of us is interconnected, woven together like threads on a loom, making our lives beautiful textiles. Some threads may never meet, but yet they all play a part in creating the textile. Whether we know it or not, we depend on and are influenced by others. That affects how the final garment looks and feels. The garment represents us, who we are, and how we choose to live and express ourselves."

"Such beautiful imagery. I gather that this philosophy inspired your new collection, We Are One."

"Indeed, my apologies if I've made this overly complex. I'm multi-sensory and not everyone should be expected to follow my thread of consciousness." She chuckles at her own pun.

"I have no doubt that a lot of our followers are right there with you. We're all so excited to witness the exclusive launch of your new line."

Maarlee smiles to encourage her guest to continue.

"I shall explain more about my garments then. This piece, like the rest in the collection, is made from textiles and decorative items found all over the world, some going back centuries. They're all carefully taken apart, cleaned, restored, and reassembled in all kinds of wonderful ways by our very talented team of designers."

"Tell us about the incredible broach your wearing and about the necklace and earrings we have here at the studio." Maarlee requests.

"To make the *ensemble* truly spectacular, every garment is coupled with a unique soul."

Maarlee touches her heart and mouths, "Wow, a soul."

"This particular kind of soul manifests in the form of divine jewelry."

Pause ...

Wonder if Jazz follows her? If not, she's going to 'flip out' with this episode, she loves fashion and artsy stuff.

Start ...

"I see what you mean; these pieces are spectacular." Maarlee's oculars show us that the objects are comprised of all kinds of intricate little details. That's way too much minutia for me.

"Our audience will appreciate you and your collection all the more when they find out that part of the proceeds of this line will support children's rights organizations around the world."

Pause ...

With every word, I understand why thousands upon thousands have tuned in; this woman is so interesting and so inspiring. Glad I was motivated to watch today.

Play ...

"Maarlee, I must say, this 3DD3 Studio Effect of yours is fabulous. Here we are, sitting together, chatting over a spot of tea, even though you're somewhere on Planet Earth, and I'm ... well, here!" Ms. Zahav points at the very comfortable looking purple chair she's sitting in.

"Would you care to share where you are today?"

"Absolutely, I'm on an island in The Caribbean, waiting for tonight's sunset performance to begin."

We see a gorgeous panoramic of a deserted beach.

"That looks just like ... What island are you on exactly?"

"I'm on The Providenciales."

"Wow, Turks and Caicos! Can't possibly improve on that location, can we guys? Well ... unless it was Maui."

Laughter from the crew erupts from the background. There's no telling where they are. They could just as easily be in someone's basement or a supermarket's warehouse. The spontaneity is what makes the show so popular. Maarlee doesn't hide anything from her audience, well, except maybe for her location.

"So happens, I was in Maui for last night's sunset. Maui is where my soul lives." A single tears rolls down her right cheek.

"*Mahalo* for being in Maui, it's magnificent. Isn't it? So happens my mother's ancestors are from the Hawaiian Islands. There is so much beauty and culture everywhere you look."

"I did a bit of research to surprise you, dear. So happens, Maui is my favorite place on Earth. I'm a big fan of your work Maarlee. Your ancestor's land continues to be a great source of inner peace and inspiration for me. It's truly paradise."

The camera shows Maarlee smiling from ear to ear and asks, "Tell us about this gorgeous book you sent."

"Before I tell you about the book, please accept it as a thank you for being a role model to young people and to many adults, who like myself, watch you loyally. You are consistently positive, and you always find ways of sharing beauty and light by being encouraging, inspiring, and supportive of children and teens' efforts."

Maarlee receives the compliments humbly in silence.

"May I take this opportunity to speak directly to your audience?"

Maarlee must trust her completely, she agrees by nodding.

"These are very challenging times for all of us, but especially for those of you designed to be exceptional human beings. You deserve the best, and because of that, you need to hear what a successful adult life looks like. Success isn't measured by fame or fortune; rather, it's measured by how we treat others and how we can contribute towards their lives. One way to start on this path is by trying this exercise tonight. Review what you accomplished today. Was it beneficial to anyone else other than yourself? Did you hurt someone unintentionally, and can you repair it? Were you a giver or a taker? If you were a taker, was it to develop something to give to others in the future?"

Ms. Zahav tears start to show, I feel some of my own.

Pause ...

She's speaking directly to me. My heart is beating fast.

Play …

"Please learn to listen to your heart. For those of you too young to know what that means … You will soon have to listen to your body's natural signals — that's known as intuition. Develop your own unique heart language. If you wish to contribute to the world, do so, but make sure it benefits those around you, don't do it just to make yourself look good or feel better."

Pause …

This is so much to process — but I have to.

Chimes …

Start …

Maarlee speaks almost in a whisper as if no one else is present. Tears continue to flow down her face.

"Thank you, Ms. Zahav, for your inspiring words and for how you live your life. We all needed to hear this today. You have changed our lives for the better."

"I simply adore kids. It's the least I can do to …" She stops because she's choking up.

Maar picks up on it and shifts, "Let's read a question from our audience. "Your name is dazzling, what does it mean and what language is it in?"

"Zivah means radiance, brilliance, light, Zahav is gold; both are Hebrew words. The two 'H's inspired my business name for which I designed the logo."

"Your quite humble Ms. Zahav, 'Home Haven' is far from being just a business, it's … an empire. You're the leader in the Fashion and Interior Design industries. Your views of the world are beyond compare. Despite your success, you don't lose sight of what's important by advocating for children across the world. That's why I consider you my role model." Maarlee proclaims.

The guest bows her head and puts her right hand on her heart, expressing gratitude with more glistening tears.

"You'll be amused to know that someone used to refer to me as his Princess Queen. Is that humble enough?" She lets out a wonderful laugh; Maar joins in.

Pause …

Wait … That laugh … where have I heard that laugh?

Play ...

Maarlee continues, "Back to your book entitled A to ZZ, it's exquisitely presented. Tell us about the cover ... the images are flat but feel raised off the surface when I touch them. Is it possible that I'm sensing ... things?"

Maarlee closes her eyes and seems transported.

"Are you alright, dear?" Ms. Zahav asks, looking intrigued.

"Yes, very much so ... I can smell the ocean by touching the image." Maarlee responds, opening her eyes. "This is incredible. The periwinkle blue sky and the aquamarine water feel cool to the touch while the coral clouds in the sunset feel warmer, and so does the sand!" Maarlee says, looking up in total astonishment.

"Now ... open it." The guest instructs.

Maarlee opens the book and gasps. "This is just beyond incredible. It's deliciously luscious."

Ms. Zahav explains, "This book is my life's work, well, at least, so far."

The audience sees a collection of notes and images, photos, and drawings of architecture, fashion sketches with snippets of fabrics and beads. In another section, there are pieces of tile and stone and metal. It's what Jazz would refer to as a sensory feast. Without hesitation, I capture the book so that I can get it for Jazz. She'll flip over it. It's the perfect gift to celebrate our life's work together. What would I ever do without her? How could I ever thank her for everything she's done and what I hope she'll continue to do for me?

Wind Chimes ...

Ms. Zahav continues, "It's been my dream to create a multi-dimensional scrapbook that expresses all my thoughts. My adventures are reflected in my work. It was just a matter of time until technology could catch up with my imagination. How else could I possibly open the windows into my creative process?"

"What a wonderful way to show us what has inspired you to design these incredible properties around the globe and the clothing line we've been talking about today."

Maarlee is overtaken by emotion; her oculars start distorting our view with her tears. She must be crying because it's so beautiful. The producer softens the sound and switches over to show many more messages cascading in.

The camera cuts back to the guest, who says, "Such a sensitive dear soul, you are Maarlee dear.

My heart is overflowing, seeing how touched you are."

Maarlee manages to say through sobs, "I can feel everything as it were real, the dimension and coolness of the pieces of tile and the texture and warmth of the fabrics."

Zivah Zahav smiles with sparkling eyes. "Graphene ... the magic comes from combining your implanted nanotechnology with graphene. It maximizes synesthetic impressions."

Pause ...

Graphene, I've always liked the sound of that word, I'm intrigued by its molecular configuration. All those hexagons coming together remind me of honeycombs and the strength that comes in numbers. Synaesthesia — I wish I were more tuned in with those sensations. I guess that's not part of my personality.

I sit up in bed and shout out. "That's it!"

That's how we're going to do it. We're going to promote the strength that comes in numbers for a common goal. We'll find ways to get signals, even if we don't have implants. We're going to get rid of The Evil Chancellor one way or another.

Play ...

"Wonderful, isn't it? Please do call me Zivah; it makes me feel even more connected to you."

"Thank you ... Zivah, I'm honored. What can you tell us about this wonderful picture on the cover?"

"Ahh ... yes, the sunset picture ... it's never been published nor seen by the public until now. It's very near and dear to my heart; its time has come. The brief version is that on my first visit to the South Pacific, I was with a group of friends. We arrived just in time to drive to the beach and watch the sunset. This photo is a souvenir of a life-altering event. Ever since then, I make sure to stop what I'm doing no matter where I am, to witness that day's sunset."

"That sounds rather intriguing. Is there any romance in the story, by chance?"

Zivah hesitates a bit before she speaks again, "Umm ... Let's save that for a conversation after the show, shall we?"

"Absolutely," Maarlee responds.

Pause ...

Wait-a-minute . . ! Is that the same image that's on Jazz's bedroom wall? It can't be..!

Rewind ...

I freeze the image and zoom in. Yup, it's the same one.

"Could Jazz gain access to this woman's private collection of photographs? Jazz is a wizard with technology, but she'd never do anything like this, or would she?" I say out loud as if Maarlee could hear me.

Bleep!

Stop jumping to unfounded conclusions.

Stop. Focus. Watch.

Start ...

We can hear a smile in the producer's voice. "Ok! We're off the air... great show, ladies!"

Oh, no! Suspecting Jazz and drifting off into thoughts of her being a hacker made me miss the rest of the interview. Darn, serves me right! That's what happens when I don't stay in the moment. I'll have to watch it again later to make sure I'm not hallucinating this whole thing. This day has had enough weird images.

Wait ... It just hit me. I recognize today's guest's laughter — it's Jazz's.

I use her words and now someone else is using her laughter? What's going on with the system today? I pull on my hair out of frustration and see loose strands stuck between my fingers. I shake them onto the floor.

Bleep!

Stop now! Breathe one ... two ... three ... Emerald.

I've got to stay focused and figure this out. Knowing Maarlee and Zivah will be speaking again shortly, I act on impulse. I send Maarlee's producer a bubblegram that says, "Great show, need to contact Maarlee asap if not sooner!" It's flagged as urgent.

My heart is pounding like crazy while I'm trying to sort this out. What will I say to Maar when she does respond?

Bleep!

Stop. Breathe. Watch.

Play ...

Great, the after-show is on.

Zivah says, "Maarlee, are you still available for a few minutes after you wrap up with production, darling?"

"Yes, of course," she responds with trepidation.

"Are you pleased with how the show turned out?"

"Oh my, very pleased, I could have gone on for days."

Maarlee glows with relief. "Let me take care of a few details and … Oops, sorry, my producer has just shown me an urgent message. I'll get back in touch shortly!"

"I'll be here … watching tonight's sunset on the island." Zivah replies with her lovely accent.

The screen transitions to a charcoal sketch of Maarlee wearing a wreath of fresh leaves and tropical flowers on her hair. The privileged access has been cut short — because of me.

"Darn!"

"Jess, is everything okay?" Maarlee sounds concerned.

"Is there another WLC atrocity I need to know about?"

This is the first time I've ever heard her unnerved.

"Hey Maar, no, nothing like that. Sure didn't mean to make you cut the after-show short. I didn't want to upset you. You know me, Ms. Impulsivity 2041; I felt something and boom, I wrote."

"So what's so urgent then?" She sounds annoyed.

"Bottom line, I may know that woman's daughter."

"What do you mean? Who's daughter?"

"I think I know Zivah's daughter," I respond.

"How do you even know she has a daughter?" Maarlee responds loudly.

A loud "shhh" comes from her producer.

I switch to whispering, "Those two have a connection, I just know it."

"Who are 'they'?" Maarlee presses, lowering her tone.

I start talking faster than ever before in my life. "Okay ... here goes ... My best friend Jazz, you know, the one that lives across the street, she could very well be Zivah's long lost daughter. She's adopted, she loves fashion and jewelry, speaks with all kinds of accents, especially a British one and her hair, it's just like Zivah's. And when Jazz laughs that same laugh, the world laughs with her, it's a wonderful laugh, isn't it? It's the best laugh."

"Whoa, slow down, Ms. Impulsivity 2041, take a breath. Your great investigative reporting isn't based on facts, is it? Thanks for the elaborate joke, Jess. You almost had me there. Gotta go." She says, brushing me off.

"No, wait, listen, don't go, please. Granted, all the other stuff could be a coincidence, but what about the large photo over Jazz's bed?"

"What large photo?"

"It's the same one as the book's cover," I exclaim.

"Oh ... c'mon, Jess, that can't be! Zivah said it was unpublished, and she wouldn't lie about that. Besides, there are so many photos of beaches out there, maybe ..."

"No!" I interrupt, "I'm not implying she lied. A photo used for a book cover would have had some details cropped. If you look at the lower-left corner, there's a surfboard fin barely showing. That's not a professional picture; that detail was left there for a reason. I just know it!"

"What're you saying?" She's frustrated

"I don't know what I'm saying, maybe I'm exercising my intuition muscle for the first time now that our implants are going to be disabled. I felt this sense of urgency and had to share it with you immediately before you speak with Zivah again."

"Jess, I know that it's tough for you to process feelings, so I appreciate that you want to act on them, but in this case ..."

I interrupt again. "Could you ask her something

like Zivah, do you have a daughter you may have given up for adoption?"

"You're kidding, right?" Maarlee responds abruptly.

"No, I'm not kidding." I snap back.

"That approach may work in the mock trials we're in, but it's not the best way to make someone feel comfortable enough to open up about their private life. I'll find a way to ask, but only if it's appropriate. I'll report later."

"Maar, sorry, I'm crazy frazzled, you're right. I'm confused, nervous, and excited all at the same time. You're great at what you do, so go do it."

"I knew you were impulsive, but I didn't know you had such a vivid imagination to go with it. Love you anyway."

Did I just make a total fool of myself? Wait, did she say she loved me? I've never heard that from anyone except my parents. When I've said it back, it's been automatic, without feelings. The only feelings I'm in touch with are indignation and frustration. Once our implants are disabled, I'm going to be a complete emotional mess. I don't need to use much imagination to figure that out.

Just as I reach to yank on my hair again …

Bleep!

Stop. Breathe. Repeat the following … I feel relaxed when …

I close my eyes and begin. "When I see emerald green, when I hear the wind rustling through leaves, when the sun shines through leaves, when the sun is on my face, when the spheres dance to music, when I get the scent of warm butter and cinnamon sugar."

I feel bathed with unfamiliar calm.

Chimes …

I dictate into a pale pink sphere.

Title: Army Of Bees Dethrone The World Chancellor.

Logo: Hexagons to resemble beehive or graphene's molecular configuration.

Colors: black, gold and something 1970's.

"I know you'll do a fab job. Love you lots, JS."

Whoosh …

The pale pink sphere zooms back much faster than expected.

"Anything the Queen Bee requests. Buzzing with anticipation! Love you lots back, JR."

On this horrible day of days, I'm finding out that my friends love me. I exhale like never before and feel motivated for tonight.

I dictate …

1) What happens once implants are 100% inactive?

2) What coping mechanisms will be available for emotional management?

3) What ….

Maar's pineapple gold sphere drifts in.

"Jess … your intuition is alive and well! There is a daughter about our age. Can't talk now … talk later!"

I'm trembling all over. My wall fades and emerald green letters appear in the most beautiful font ever.

Congratulations, Jessica Stafford!
You are developing feminine intuition.

Me developing anything feminine sounds like an absolute miracle.

Chimes …

I learned so much from Zivah Zahav today without even realizing it. Doing one thing at a time and listening to others, observing their body language and mannerisms proved to be very helpful.

This is huge — The Scarsdale Self Proclaimed Know It All is evolving! None of these insights would be possible if I weren't interested in helping my best friend. With this new awareness, I could change people's lives, or better yet, I could change the world!

Chimes ...

This is so exciting! I need to tell Jazz immediately. She'll be pleased to know that I'm becoming more intuitive and less self-absorbed!

Bleep!

Stop.

Oops, yeah, can't, poor timing. Forget it, self-awareness is too hard.

Bleep!

Focus. Be patient.

Weighing the possibilities, buying the book would give Jazz so much pleasure, but it's a risky move that could hurt more people than it would help, especially her parents. Jazz knows she's adopted, but maybe not much else, we've never talked about it. Maybe because she already knows Zivah? A few years ago, she started doing her hair differently for a special occasion, and it looked like Zivah's. At about that same time, she changed the way she spells her name. It went from Jasmin to Jazzmyn with double z's — Zivah Zahav has double …

Chimes …

I wonder if Jazz's parents know she knows, that is if she knows. It could be a coincidence or a teenage phase.

The Ross's have helped me widen what otherwise would be a very narrow view of the world. My life had consisted of riding the train from Scarsdale to New York and back for high school debates. Then it was upgraded by flying out-of-state, to argue and win prizes. Has any of that had an impact on the world? Right now, all that my arguing gets me is a lot of trouble. So, to stay out of trouble, I spend a lot of time in Jazz's house where I can talk about anything. No subject is controversial or off-limits.

Listening to her parents' passionate views and how they resolve their differences has allowed me to develop my own opinions. As a result, I can be much more effective in whatever I choose to take on. I don't know what brought them to live in Scarsdale, especially on this side of the tracks, but I'm eternally grateful.

The Ross's have worked so hard to help orphaned children around the world. I remember asking Mr. Ross when I was much younger, "Wouldn't it be great if all the children that get adopted didn't have to travel halfway across the world to meet their new parents?"

"What do you mean?" He seemed genuinely intrigued.

"What if they could walk in one door and come out another, and the parents would be waiting for them, no passports needed."

Jazz chimed in, "If that would happen, then anyone could have the freedom to travel anywhere, whenever they wanted to."

What a fun conversation that was.

Bleep!

Important Notice — As implants start to lose reserve, unrelated thoughts or other's thoughts may filter through from person to person.

Now that's funny. My thoughts bounce around like that all the time. Maybe being on a low reserve won't seem that unfamiliar to me. I have got to stop thinking thoughts. I'm exhausted. The only way I can take a break from myself is to visit Samson even if it's in my imagination.

What a great idea … Samson is going to be the main character in my paper for Mrs. García.

I start dictating …

Samson and I have the perfect relationship. He's older than I am, wise, strong, but also gentle; always available and expects nothing back. He holds me and makes me feel safe and calm. Being with him allows my mind and my body to slow down. Samson doesn't live very far away at all. In fact, he lives in our backyard. Samson is my favorite tree. He lets me climb up, one branch at a time.

We have a ritual, Samson and I. When I reach his canopy; I close my eyes, take a deep breath, and repeat my mantra.

Emerald … one … two … three …

Sometimes I'm up there for hours and lose track of time.

"Jess?" Mom calls from downstairs. "Dinner's ready, sweetie."

Meaning, you snooze, you lose. Mom likes for us to eat at the same time every day, three times a day. With Jake and his voracious appetite, there are no leftovers if I don't make it to the table on time.

"Coming in five," I respond as I dictate the closing paragraph of my assignment.

I look out the window and see that today's beautiful daylight is fading. That large star that broke through the dense morning haze is now looking rather tired, ready to make its departure. Our blazing globe perseveres though not everyone appreciates the light he emits. Without accepting defeat, he helps create striking abstract paintings with phenomenal colors. What a beautiful way of bidding farewell.

"*Voila* …!"

My thoughts shift to Zivah Zahav. Wouldn't she make an incredible mentor? My theories about her possible connection to Jazz wouldn't have to come up; they're only my crazy theories, after all. She could teach me how to have an incredible life and how to create a safer and more beautiful planet for us to live on.

I grab my body pillow, snuggle up, and close my eyes.

I need to rest for just a few. I drift off, saying …

Emerald … One … two … three …

A loud twang, much like that of an electric guitar startles me. An image drifts in on my Glåsse, it's Tomas Kesher looking troubled.

years

"How many times have I told you to forbid the children from speaking while I'm driving. I find their ridiculous helium chatter insufferable." He proclaims in that typical condescending tone.

"What a cold-hearted person you are," I reply, trying hard to hold back tears.

Without changing expression, he raises the volume of his musical selection.

I've asked myself over and over, throughout the years how did I end up marrying this man? One who prefers listening to Wagnerian opera over the sound of his own toddlers' darling conversations. Today, driving back from the airport with my now teenagers, I'm experiencing newfound bliss. I should feel guilty, but instead, I feel relieved.

He's gone, he's actually — gone.

The signs were all there, but I didn't have the life experience to recognize them. I was a naive, sheltered book smart young woman who could only think about two things, studying at La Sorbonne and that Jonathan seemed to 'like' me.

Back then, Jonathan was handsome and a touch too arrogant for most. He was well-read in just about every subject, and his superpower was making molecular biology look like fine art and sound like poetry. As a group of students, we'd get together after hours to have passionate discussions with him; they always seemed to reach a crescendo at around midnight. We'd speak about anything and everything, from Shakespeare to DNA to the chemistry of French Cuisine. I was mesmerized and couldn't get enough of his brilliance. He was like a drug I needed to consume as often as possible. Without realizing it, I had fallen captive to the charms of my university professor's assistant.

One day after class, he insinuated we go out.

"What you're suggesting is against school regulations, isn't it?

Students and teachers fraternizing?" I inquired.

"Not really … considering I'm not a full-blown professor and with my expert tutelage, you'll complete this class before everyone else does. If we're discreet and you tell no one, we should be fine. Accept?"

Looking back, his words came across all too well scripted. How many times had he said the same thing to other starry-eyed female students? It may have seemed that I followed his instructions obediently, but I did confide in my roommates.

Anamaría was an olive-skinned, dark-haired, passionate beauty from Spain. Britt, her counterpart from Norway, was an exquisitely tall, fair-featured and fair-minded, mature young woman.

They were so much more experienced in life and well versed in healthy dating vs. sick dating than I. Coming from a conservative environment, I thought dating was the necessary process to find a spouse. I never knew it was considered a fun sport. They strongly encouraged me to stop seeing him.

"Please, Paula, reconsider before it's too late. You are such a desirable woman. Why are you giving all your energy and attention to him?" Britt demands.

"Why not let highly desirable men approach you?" Ana wants to know.

"What highly desirable men?" I ask.

"You haven't noticed that Gio Guarnieri is extremely interested in you?" Ana pushes. "I hope someday someone looks at me the way he looks at you."

"I'm only interested in developing a relationship with one person at a time and that person is Jonathan," I respond much to my friends' dismay.

"He really has you under a spell." Britt shares sadly.

Ana's response is a litany of story after story filled with painful examples of 'don't ever date staff' and the brutal aftermath. They both know Jonathan's reputation around campus focuses on his ego and controlling women.

One evening, after a long sleep-deprived study session, I suggest, "Let's go get ice cream sundaes, the sugar and the dairy should knock us out in no time."

My determined roommates are on a mission to make me come to my senses, even while we're enjoying our sundaes.

"Paula, think about it, he doesn't have any men friends, and he always surrounds himself with students. That's an important indicator." Britt determined.

"I've told you both; I don't want to stop seeing him because he says he thinks he may love me." I offered. "Besides, breaking up would upset him, and that would ruin my grades for the semester, not to mention my life. My goal is to complete a Ph.D. and work with NASA."

Ana looks at Britt as they shake their heads in unison.

"Paula, do you not hear yourself? You're putting him first." Comes from Britt.

Ana exclaims in full *Madrileña* mode. *"¿Qué os pasa mujer, os habéis vuelto loca?"*

"No Ana, *no estoy loca*, I'm not crazy, I'm in love with him."

There, I had said it. My decisions were based purely on feelings and not on facts. A total contradiction to how scientists process information.

"Very well then, under the circumstances, from this day forward, we proclaim you to be our Royal Queen," Anamaría announces.

"What an honor. Is it because of my elegant demeanor, impeccable presence, and strong convictions for what I think is right?" I ask.

"¡Lo siento, pero no! It's short for Queen of Denial." Ana laughs.

I feel hurt and respond, "You should be more open-minded. Behind that 'know it all' attitude is a sensitive guy with a great sense of humor who's allowed me into his inner sanctum. When I've asked why he doesn't show that side to others, he's explained that no one would take him seriously and that laughing makes one vulnerable."

"He is brilliant. He's found his perfect victim because you refuse to see him for who he really is." Britt clarifies.

Had I only listened to my wise friends back then, my life would have turned out quite differently. In my mind, only beautiful things could happen in perfect weather like we had that fateful Friday morning.

A freshman knocked on my door, announcing that Jonathan was waiting for me in the courtyard. I was so excited that taking an extra minute to change out of my pajamas and robe would have been too long. How could I make him wait if he was being spontaneous? There he was, more handsome than ever, dressed in a suit and tie, holding a bounty of multicolor roses.

"Good Morning Paula. After much deliberation, I've decided it's time to settle down with a woman who fulfills all my requirements. In my estimation, that would be you. You've proven capable of keeping up with your workload and my considerable intellect."

I was shaking inside like a leaf. I was ecstatic. Out of the corner of my eye, I saw students starting to congregate around us. Was a flash mob about to burst out in song and dance for us? What a ridiculous idea.

Jonathan handed me the bouquet and looked me over head to toe, because I was barefoot. "You're an attractive woman despite your current attire; so genetically and statistically speaking, we should have above-average looking children with above-average intelligence."

"Thank you for the academic assessment, professor." Before I could put the bouquet down, an unknown lady-in-waiting grabbed it away from me.

"Paula Kesher, will you marry me?" He asked.

Since I was known for my quick wit, I was trying hard to come up with something clever to say, but all that came out was, "Yes, I will."

Good thing so many 'attendants' were filming from all angles. I wanted to have a record of every detail of that fine day. Disproportionate amounts of applause and cheering erupted. He cut through the noise by projecting his best professorial voice for everyone to hear. "I have three rings selected. I want you to choose the one you like best."

He got closer and whispered, "The jeweler is expecting us at 4:00 pm this afternoon."

"So much for free will," I whispered back, giggling.

He said nothing and kissed the base of my ring finger. It may have appeared to be romantic, but now I realize it was all an act.

Years later, I was persuaded to attend a class reunion at Anamaría's and Britt's insistence. With a double scoop of ice cream before me, I finally had the courage to tell my friends the truth.

"My married life … has been quite difficult. You were both right. The realization started to sink in before our civil marriage."

Ana is incensed. "What do you mean? Why didn't you tell us?"

"There would've been time to back out, at the last minute, even then." Britt shares.

"I didn't know how to. I never knew what to expect from him. Sometimes he'd brush the most serious things off as if they were nothing. He would never blow up when I was prepared for it. Other times, he'd have a disproportionate reaction to the smallest of things. I walked on eggshells for twenty long years, it was emotionally exhausting."

"What do you mean by that?" Ana inquires leaning forward.

"Well, for example, when we were about to get married, I brought up the subject of my last name. To hyphen or not to hyphen? His response was that no one in the world of academia bothered with that convention. He felt that having to prove one is married with a name change was *passé* and quite beneath me. I rationalized it by convincing myself there'd be one less thing on my long 'to do' list. You know how much I love making lists and crossing things off, right?"

Ana puts her hands to the sides of her head in shock and shakes it. "I would have walked out right then and there."

"You experienced this next one at the university, it was consistent throughout his life. When it came to being on time … he wasn't. He acted as if it was an honor for others to wait by keeping their business open late, just for him. In fact, the day we went to the justice of the peace, we arrived five minutes before closing."

"I gather that since you knew we weren't his greatest fans, you were forced not to invite us to your religious wedding. *¿Cierto?*" Ana surmises.

I responded tearfully, "*No, no es cierto*, there was no other wedding, Ana."

"What do you mean? No religious wedding? That was so important to you and your family?" Ana raises her voice and bangs on the table.

Britt motions her to calm down, people in other tables are turning around to look.

"I was very naive about glossing over the consequences of our different backgrounds. He was unwilling to have a wedding or a life with what he referred to as spiritual representation. He frowned upon my family's traditions and managed to spin a complex web of isolation around me. He forbade me from being in contact with everyone I had ever known."

"What about his own family?" They asked in unison.

"He had an explanation for everything, so after a while, I dropped it."

"What about your honeymoon?" Ana chimes in.

"No honeymoon either, *amigas*." I feel so embarrassed.

"I knew he was manipulative, but I had no idea of the extent of his cruelty. I'm truly sorry, Paula. I should have been much more firm with you." Britt says with tears in her large crystalline blue eyes.

"Lo siento en el alma." Anita starts sobbing.

We lose sight of where we are. We hug and cry as a single soul.

After the banquet ends, my friends and I go back to the hotel where my saga continues.

"Do you feel strong enough to watch some footage we managed to confiscate from that fateful Friday morning?" Britt asks cautiously.

"You might as well exorcise this whole thing out of me. I owe it to myself and to my children. By the way, I never asked. Where were you both that weekend?"

"We were treated to a statistics conference, courtesy of Jonathan. He had thought of everything. He knew we would have prevented you from saying yes." Britt explains.

"I would have resorted to kidnapping," Ana adds.

"Anita, if you had, I wouldn't have had my two children."

"Tenéis razón, amiga." She replies.

"Very well, as your fellow scientists aka exorcists, we shall initiate the arduous procedure to remove this darkness from within you, once and for all." Britt declares.

"You're safe with us Paulita, we love you and always will." Ana shares as they both hug and kiss me.

Britt unravels her Intellitela and the footage begins. As a spectator, I realized that the whole proposal had been cold and impersonal. Most painful of all, the word 'love' didn't have a part in this farce nor in our entire relationship. He knew that the magic words I needed to hear to fall in his final trap were: you're intelligent and you're attractive. Though I was flying high, my self-esteem was much lower than I realized.

Britt explained, "Jonathan strongly encouraged people to witness the event in exchange for the promise of scholastic perks."

"He resorted to bribery too?" I exclaim.

Ana adds, "I got the flash mob captain to confess that they were all hoping you'd decline the proposal. That would have been enough of a reward for them."

"He remembered that from twenty years ago?" I remark.

"Yes, to this day. He's here for the reunion, too." Ana shares.

"People liked you a great deal and still do, Paula.

You were always so upbeat and clever. No one understood why you'd choose to marry him." Britt explains.

"In an odd way, knowing that helps even after all this time." I tear up.

I explained that while I was working hard at school, he started pursuing positions in the US that would offer an excellent salary. He reassured me that I could always find a small laboratory close by and continue 'doing my little experiments' if I wanted. I had to keep that all to myself.

"Continue doing your 'little' experiments? Didn't he know you were applying at NASA?" Ana interjects.

"He could be funny so I thought he was kidding. I even asked him jokingly who'd commute to work, him or me? He became silent and replied he wasn't expecting such insolence from me."

"Insolence?" Ana and Britt repeat in unison.

"Sorry to ask, but I must know, did he ever hurt you physically?"

"No Britt, too cowardly. He excelled at hurting us with words. He was constantly putting us down, especially the kids. He kept me in a constant state of implied threats."

"What would he threaten you with?" Ana asks in disbelief.

"When we'd get into discussions he'd say things like …" I pause.

"It's okay, please go on." Britt says reassuringly as she reaches for my hand.

"He threatened by saying he'd tell people that if I left him, he'd explain that I'd had a nervous breakdown and been confined to a mental institution. After all, who'd ever believe my side of what he was really like."

Ana lets out a string of *Madrileña* expletives.

"He really had no insight whatsoever into his own behavior, did he? A classic case of Narcissism." Britt determines.

"Precisely, but anyway … time passed with school and work. Waiting for responses distracted me from my growing mental list of resentments towards him."

"Now I understand why you never explored leaving him." Britt states.

"Glad you do because I can't fully understand it myself."

"It was part of his tangled web. He was very

seductive in his own twisted way. He perfected his techniques down to a science." Britt clarifies.

I burst out into tears that had accumulated inside of me for what seemed an eternity. Even though I was tired of talking, I knew we had to continue. The so-called exorcism went on for most of the night and into the next morning.

"A cold and dreary French afternoon brought exciting news; my dream had come true! We'd have to splurge and go out for dinner to celebrate. For once, I couldn't wait for Jonathan to get home. When he opened the door, he was beaming, so rare for him, especially with such weather."

"Did he find out about your acceptance?" Ana asks optimistically.

I shake my head and continue recounting, "Paula ... darling ... great news!!" His words echoed in our sparsely furnished apartment.

"I know, I know!" I said, walking towards him.

"You already know?" He asked.

"Of course I do, silly!"

"Can you believe it? I've been invited to be a professor at a prestigious university in upstate New York. Such a phenomenal opportunity for me. No more limbo, the decision has been made.

We're moving back to The States!" He hugged me and lifted me off the ground.

"But …"

"I know, you're wondering what if the NASA thing goes through, what then? Face the facts, whether you're qualified or not, it's not happening, and the position will go to a man anyway."

At that moment, something shifted inside of me. My joy transformed into self-contained, fuming rage.

"It so happens they 'have' let me know." I snapped.

"See, I told you not to get your hopes up. Anyone, I know?"

"Yes, actually, you do … they've chosen me!"

Without changing expressions or missing a beat, he said, "The NASA thing is just not going to work for us, darling."

"What do you mean — for us? I've worked very hard my entire life for this moment. I won't permit you to disregard my triumph as trash!"

He smiled as if finding my reaction amusing. "Would you like me to contact them to say you are declining because of your husband's new prestigious position?"

I cut him off. I couldn't handle that arrogant tone a moment longer.

"Don't bother. I'll take care of it." I stomped out and slammed the bedroom door.

"*¡Ole!* Glad rooming with a *Madrileña* eventually paid off for you." Ana quips.

"From that day forward, I became another Paula Kesher. He never found out that NASA wanted me so badly, that they actually assembled a team of scientists outside NYC to work under my direction. Jonathan never questioned where I went to work. He didn't care."

"How did you survive emotionally?" Britt wonders.

"You know, exciting projects make up for dull lives."

Britt signals me to proceed.

"We each settled into our routines, and two years later, we had our first child. Do you remember Jonathan's theory about names? He was always adamant about calling people only by their given name; no diminutives, no terms of endearment allowed either, unless, of course, he wanted something from you." I clarify.

"I do recall when he lectured about given names, he equated them to genetic markers, no one can change them. Didn't that sound off to you?" Britt asks.

"Truthfully, I found it quirky and inconsequential until we had children. He insisted we give our daughter an androgynous name that wouldn't get in the way of her future career. Madison was an energetic bundle of joy whom I loved calling Baby Maddy when he wasn't around. She became everything I felt I wasn't, cute, sassy, overly confident, and rebellious, craving constant attention, especially from boys."

"She takes after her Tía Anamaría." Britt jokes.

"My maternal instinct was greater than my unhappiness. By the time Tomas came two years after Maddy, I had come to terms with my loveless marriage, it didn't stop me from wanting to have children. I suspect Tomas was able to pick up on my feelings in utero. This fragile little child of mine with delicate porcelain features possessed a certain sadness and intensity from the very beginning. Whereas Maddy had tremendous strength and power from the minute she came out. You can just imagine how intimidating and annoying she is to her brother. She's loud, he's quiet, she loves to dance and can strike up a conversation with a lamp post and he …"

"… Struggles with every aspect of living life?" Britt finishes my sentence.

"Exactly. You'll appreciate knowing that once Tomas was old enough, he developed great mental agility. He worked through his father's illogical pompous theories by creating some of his own. His father should have been thrilled that his progeny, who resembled him physically and intellectually, had also inherited his ability to analyze complex information. Instead, he was highly threatened."

Ana mumbles inaudibly in Spanish as Britt smiles with amusement.

"Jonathan is still holding a grudge against his son. By the time Tomas was three, his father was no longer able to manipulate him. Our toddler's intuition was much more developed than mine ever was as an adult."

"One morning over breakfast, our precocious five-year-old asked his father if he had ever considered that genetic mutations and possible alterations through robotics and implants could improve the human species. Jonathan looked at him with a glimmer of delight that quickly shifted to disdain."

"What in the world are you talking about, Tomas?" Jonathan exclaimed, leaning towards him.

"Well, Father, if we alter cells with robotics to help people feel better, we could also change their names to make them feel better."

Ana places her hands on her cheeks with delight. "*¡Ay, ya, yay!* What a delicious boy."

"Jonathan showed little interest in discussing that topic with him. He told him that as a child, he didn't have enough life experience or information to have this type of conversation with him or anyone."

Britt mumbles inaudibly in Norwegian as Ana and I nod in agreement.

"My beautiful boy looked like a piece of shattered glass, holding itself together by sheer will. Who knows how long it took him to prepare his thoughts and muster the courage to speak up at the table."

"Who in their right mind wouldn't want to hear every word coming out of that precious boy's mouth?" Ana asks.

"Tomas, finish your meal. There are children starving in ..." Jonathan said without even looking at his disappointed son.

Tomas looked down, staring at his uneaten breakfast.

"I can't do anything about children starving in another continent right now, and you can't do anything about shipping my leftovers either because we don't have any dry ice in the house." Tomas attempted to raise his shy little voice in defiance.

"Up until that day, Tomas could not speak up for himself. Though it was a very painful experience, I was so proud of him but had to keep the celebration to myself."

Maddy, on the other hand, burst out laughing. "Now that's your best one yet, TomTom!"

"Both of you are disappointments to me. I don't find your comments at all humorous. Leave the table at once!" Jonathan demands.

The kids go to their rooms and slam their doors at the same time.

"Great way of dealing with your own low self-esteem, professor. You'll get 'Father of the Year Award' for this one." I mumbled and left the room.

I explained that less than a month later, The Controller In Chief or TCC, as the kids referred to him, announced that he'd been offered a prestigious position back at La Sorbonne.

Ana puts her palms together and looks up, *"Gracias, Dios mío."*

"I was not about to leave my work nor uproot my children, but he never asked. Had he asked, I would have declined without hesitation. He must have realized that he'd reached the end of the line with all of us. This was his perfect out because his fragile ego would be intact. I didn't have to deal with any more drama. Though he had ample time to prepare for his departure, he told the faculty at the university that he was needed immediately. Without any fanfare and no tears from us, he left. The kids agreed to go to the airport. He thought they wanted to say their goodbyes."

"Did he really get a position at La Sorbonne?" Britt inquires.

"I chose not to ask," I explain.

"At the airport, Jonathan asked Tomas to shake his hand before he boarded."

"You'll be the man of the house in my absence. I'm counting on you to look after your mother and sister. I'll be gone for long stretches but could arrange a trip back, but only if I'm not too busy."

"Tomas responded by looking away and putting both hands in his pockets. Maddy stayed busy on her device. The kids did look at him, but only to make sure he entered the gate. On the way back, Tomas had a highly explosive, delayed reaction to his father's parting words."

"Oh please! Who was this last little performance at the airport for? Any students around to impress? You're counting on me? You've never included me in anything. How can you count on someone you've always treated like a zero to the left? You've never shown me any respect." He takes a breath and goes on. "Hope you bought a one-way ticket for Europe. Hope you don't ever come back!"

"I was stunned to realize that my son had more to say."

"You keep telling me I'm weak and not in touch with my feelings. What do you know about feelings? I'm quite in touch with mine and you know what they're saying? They're saying … I hate you!" Tomas yelled out, using every ounce of energy he possessed.

"With that declaration, it started pouring rain, making visibility from the van, impossible. When I get anxious, knots form in my head and stomach, and I feel pressure in my chest. I'm frazzled, I need to pull over for our safety and to try to appease my children. Every time it thundered, it seemed Tomas' rage escalated. Maddy couldn't contain herself any longer and burst into tears. Her brother stopped ranting long enough to say, 'What do you have to cry about, Ms. Wonder Woman? Since when do you have any feelings or care about anything or anybody other than yourself? You're just like him!'"

"You don't know what you're talking about, so just shut up!" His sister yells out.

"Tomas, Madison, enough!" I yell as I'm pulling into a parking lot.

Tomas keeps going, "I know a lot more than you'll ever know because I'm much smarter than you are. All you care about is hair, makeup, clothes and that empty-headed jock, Jake Stafford. Why do you have a crush on someone too stupid to tie his own shoes? Lucky for you, he ignores you just like the other guys do."

"Tomas Kesher!" I yell again, "That's not acceptable — apologize right now!"

"Why should I apologize for telling the truth? You know I never lie."

"Poor Maddy starts hyperventilating. Even if it's pouring, I get out of the driver's seat, open her side of the car and hop in, soaking wet. I sit between them and place my arm around her."

"Put your head down between your knees; that's it. Breathe sweetheart … In ... Out ... Again."

"Tomas stops raging long enough to start hitting the back of the passenger seat like a punching bag. In the middle of that nightmare, I feared what Jonathan would say when he saw the damage to the car seat."

"What?" Ana exclaims.

"I know, it's hard to believe, but at that moment, when my children were in crisis, I completely forgot he was gone. I was still afraid of what he was going to say. He'd probably say something profoundly cruel to Tomas."

"It takes years and years to break the cycle." Britt shares knowingly.

"What cycle are you talking about?" Ana asks, suspecting Britt knows more about the situation than she does.

I nod back and proceed with my long story.

Maddy starts to open up. "I feel the same way Tomas does — I hate him too! I'm so tired of pretending to be somebody I'm not. Tomas, you think I don't care about anything or anybody. I care and a lot more than you realize. I'm an outstanding actress." She says between sobs.

"He would have picked on you even more if I hadn't been around to distract him."

The punching stops. "What do you mean?" He asks.

"The most crucial factors in life for TCC are genetics and intelligence, right? So instead of competing with his mental grandiosity, I kept getting back at him by acting dumb and superficial. Imagine his shame; having an airhead for a daughter. Such sweet revenge."

Tomas interrupts, "I always wondered how you got such good marks in school, I always thought you were cheating."

"Thanks a lot, snob." She kicks the back of the driver's seat since she can't get to him otherwise.

"Kids, let's not fight, I beg of you, please."

Maddy's insights were astounding. "Once you disappoint TCC enough times or call him out on stuff, he shuts you out completely and forever. He acts politely in public, but he's not as good an actor as I am."

"What do you mean by that?" Tomas asks.

She starts sobbing again and covers her face as if feeling shame. "He's not a good person, okay, he's just not. I refused to do what he wanted, one too many times, so he cut me off. I'm telling you once you're on to him, that's it! I paid a heavy price, but it's worth it because now … I'm freeee!" She squeals.

"What was the price?" Tomas asks, trying to keep up.

"Mom, did you ever wonder why my girlfriends stopped coming over to spend time with me?" Maddy asks.

I reply cautiously. "I thought it was … sorry, son … because your brother would feel overwhelmed by so many rowdy girls at once. I thought you were being considerate of him."

Maddy clarifies, "It had nothing to do with being considerate. It was because the girls thought TCC was creepy. He always wanted to be with us, to impress us with his stuck up stories. Word got out, so they all cut me off. I don't have girlfriends anymore — thanks to him."

I'm looking down, riddled by my shame as a mother.

"Oh Maddy, honey, I don't know what to say other than please forgive me for not seeing what was going on." This was the first time I'd cried in front of them.

Tomas interrupts and shares with his sister, "If you tell your friends that TCC is gone, they might come back to see you. He was the irritant, not you — not even me. I'll even keep my door closed when they come over. They won't bother me — as much."

"Thanks, TomTom, I'll try that. Mom, you couldn't have seen it, you were working at the lab. I didn't tell you because, well … he threatened to be harder on you and Tomas. He told me not to tell anyone."

I put my arms around them both and feel Tomas stiffen up. "My precious beautiful children, I'm so sorry you've been carrying so much around for all these years. I hope you'll forgive me for not giving you the emotional space to express yourselves." We huddle, trying to cry the pain away. I cloak them with every ounce of my love.

"Mommy, I love you so much, and lots and lots more," Maddy speaks like a little girl, clinging to me like never before.

"I love you too, Mom, and the truth is, he doesn't love us or anybody," Tomas says, squeezing my hand.

Our sobs dissipate and so does the storm.

"Okay, Kesher Clan, I say we've cried enough for one day. Let's take a well-deserved break so we can make more tears when we need them again later."

The kids blow their noses.

Tomas says, "Okay, we're finished now."

"May I remind you that you inherited my sense of mischief and humor. The next best part of today is knowing that we don't have to hide that part or any part of ourselves anymore!" I announce. "That is a gift for us from above."

"The kids looked up at the roof of the car, shrugging their shoulders with confusion. First, I thought they were pretending not to know what 'from above' meant. But then I realized I'd never felt free enough to speak to them about spirituality. Finally, I was in full control to raise my children, my way." I share with relief.

Britt and Ana are listening intently.

"Who's up for a triple ice cream sundae for dinner tonight?" I ask the kids.

"We are …we are!" They both yell out like 'regular' kids.

Britt interrupts lovingly. "Paula, after what you've shared, it sounds to me that your kids are anything but regular."

"Tomas has such a knack for connecting with other brilliant kids on science platforms, like my Dahvid and your Lena." Ana turns to Britt, as her gypsy eyes sparkle with pride.

"Do your kids struggle with not being present in the moment?" I ask them both. "That's one of Tomas' biggest challenges. He's always somewhere else in his head. He prefers the big picture and runs away from details; he calls them Le Grand Minutia."

Britt giggles, "Imagine if Lena felt that way, I'd be a complete failure as a mother."

"A statistician's daughter who hates details, now that's funny," Ana says laughing out loud.

What a pleasure to hear myself laugh with my dear friends. It's been so long.

"You'll be proud of this next episode. Tomas asked me if I could help him find a part-time job recently. He wanted to buy a guitar."

"That sounds like my Dahvid is having quite an influence on him. He loves playing all kinds of guitars."

"Probably so, Anita. So do you want to know what happened next?"

My friends agree, even if by now, we're completely exhausted.

Maddy suggested they go into business together, and her brother responded, "Thanks but no way."

"She flipped her hair and pretended to leave the room, knowing he'd change his mind. She knows her brother isn't the type to mow lawns or shovel snow off sidewalks. Fortunately for him, we live in a high rise on Garth Road, so those services aren't exactly in high demand." I chuckle.

"So how did you help him make him feel he could contribute?" Britt wonders.

"First, you need to know that my son has exquisite taste in musical instruments. Shall I thank Dahvid for that too?" I say looking at Ana. "The one he chose was out of anyone's reach unless you're a famous rock star. I offered to look for something similar that wouldn't cost as much so we could afford some lessons. He thanked me and said it wasn't necessary."

"I can figure out how to play it on my own. I just need to earn enough to buy the guitar. Mom — please don't do me any favors. Okay? I want to earn it myself."

"Tomas is a gifted child with an ability to comprehend the most elevated forms of data.

He got his father's best qualities, looks, and proficiency in math. Remember how Jonathan would spend hours writing formulas on the board in class as if he were writing a long story? Well, Tomas has been doing the same thing for years with musical notes without needing an instrument."

"Remarkable." Britt and Ana respond in unison.

Britt recalls, "I do recall a particular tutoring session when Jonathan insisted, with his pedantic tone, that what he was writing was the most important story there was. It was the story of how the universe works, where there is no beginning and there's no end, it's a continuum."

I add, "… and I remember that class because he drew a shape on the board that reminded me of a nautilus shell within the confines of different sized boxes. He thought I was staring at him, but I was mesmerized by the shape. I've used The Fibonacci Spiral as a hypnotic technique to help me with anxiety and to help me sleep."

"Fascinating … Why don't you guide us through it. We need to go into a deep meditative state for an hour, otherwise, we'll miss our flights." Britt suggests with a wink as she points at Ana who's reluctantly dosing off.

A couple of hours later, as we say our goodbyes in the hotel lobby, I need to share one more thing.

"Ana, when we were in school, I envisioned you like the hot pepper I needed to spice up my dull life. Britt, you've always been so grounded and generous with your wisdom. My vision of you has always been the salt of the earth. After this weekend, you've both shown me that it's important to have a little bit of both to have a healthy balance. You'll never know how much you've helped me in the last 24 hours." We hug and shed tears of relief.

"Let's plan another getaway soon. *Las quiero muchísimo.*" I say blowing them a kiss as I get in the cab.

On the flight back, as my life's review continues, I realize that fortunately, Tomas also takes after me. He can be surprisingly funny, even if he doesn't realize it. He loves to cook and bake from scratch. That's our special time together; that's when he opens up and shares his deepest feelings. Having utensils and food in my hands prevents me from wanting to hold him when he's upset. Sometimes, I'll reach for an onion to mask my tears. He hates seeing his sister or me crying.

"Mom, I like cooking because it has nothing to do with estrogen or testosterone, it has to do with formulas and chemical reactions."

"Interesting way of introducing the subject of hormones into a conversation. Have you started discovering the joy of spending time with girls yet? Do you have any questions for me?" I ask with a rascally smile.

He rolls his eyes and continues preparing the salad.

His classmate, Jessica Stafford, is one of his obsessive topics. He seems to like her, but he's also intimidated by her.

"Tomas, teenagers are tough to figure out, especially girls and especially someone as bright as Jessica. We've talked about emotional intelligence before, right? Girls just seem to develop that part of themselves earlier."

"Wow! I finally discovered that there's one part of Madison that's underdeveloped." I start laughing before he does. It takes him longer to realize when he's said something very clever.

"From a scientific standpoint, I concur with your findings wholeheartedly!" I exclaim.

Our laughter travels throughout the apartment. Hearing my laughter in this environment is like bringing a long lost friend into my home for the first time. I've missed being with my true self. Glad I'm on my way back.

Maddy wonders in to find out what's so funny.

"We were talking about how silly girls can be," Tomas replies.

"Oh, really," Maddy says. "That's too bad. I came in to share a business proposition so you can earn the money you need to get that rock star guitar. Guess you're not interested in hearing what a silly girl has to say." She responds playfully.

"We're interested, aren't we Tomas?" I suggest gesturing for her to sit with us.

Maddy gets very serious and says, "Tomas, here's the thing, you're a really great chef and I … have a stellar personality and looks to match. So how about if we combine our talents for a win-win-win situation and help Mom too?"

"I'm listening." He responds.

She speaks quickly, Tomas tries to remain focused.

"Here's the plan, I have it all figured out. Ready? Mom, you and Tomas will come up with a menu and a profit margin. I'll do all the graphics, including the logo. Mom, you'll receive the prepaid orders so you'll know how much to buy and how much to prepare. *Voila!* They order, we shop, you cook, I deliver, you two get the profits, and I get the tips and all the attention. What do you think about that? Brilliant, right?"

Tomas stares into space and says, "I have three questions. One, how will people know about us if they've never tasted our products? Two, what are we doing for containers?"

"What's the third?" She asks.

"Three, what's the name of our new business … partner?" Tomas gives his sister a touch-free high five.

"One, that's easy, I already asked our *concierge* if we could set up a tasting party in the small conference room and he said yes. Two, we buy containers in bulk and we'll add our logo. Three, we need to come up with the name together. Any more questions from the panel?" She says flashing her great smile.

"Thank you, sweetie; you've given us food for thought," I say, getting ready to stand up, downplaying my joy.

Tomas becomes pensive again and then shares, "I like it. I like the whole thing. So I'd like to place the first order, cook us up three logos to choose from for 'Food For Thought'." Tomas seems pleased.

His sister jumps up and does her cheer routine, using several napkins in each hand as pompoms. She leaves the room, hopping and skipping.

"Mom, I don't have room in my head or energy in my body to handle a girlfriend with Wonder Woman living under our roof. Have you ever noticed that she has way too much energy and too many curves? Is that normal? Does an estrogen imbalance cause that? You're a scientist, can you do something for Maddy? Can you make some of her excesses go away?"

"That excess of estrogen contained within your sister is what helped her create a brilliant business plan for you. One where you don't have to interact with any people. Care to reconsider?"

He smirks and rolls his eyes. "Fiiine, we'll keep her as is ..."

My two children vibrate at very different frequencies, but that night they harmonized beautifully. A couple of days later, there was a definite shift in our lives. Maddy got an invitation for a sleepover from a new girl from school. Tomas suggested we celebrate by having a quiet evening, just him and I, to practice making some of our dishes. He began the process by pulling out all the measuring cups, cutting boards, knives, mixing bowls, basically every cooking utensil we owned.

"Are you using all of these tools at once?" I was intrigued.

"I don't know Mom." He snaps, looking agitated. "Right now, I need to organize the process in my head. We have to use the best tools for the best results."

"On second thought, maybe we shouldn't do this at all, too many decisions, too much work. Can we do takeout for dinner instead?" He pleads.

I've learned not to respond or react to his upsets, I simply reach for 'my' best tool. Tapping on the music icon on my Intellitela brings The Four Seasons by Vivaldi's beautiful notes to life. The kitchen starts filling with calming images. Within thirty seconds, Tomas' body posture relaxes, and he starts grouping the utensils he needs while putting away the others.

He stands back, admires his work, and kisses his fingers, *"Magnifique,* let the cooking begin!" He says with a French accent. Is Tomas learning to speak French? How delightful! Where in the world did that come from? In any event, my beautiful boy is appreciating the view of his soon-to-be scrumptious accomplishments.

"Mom, today has been a wonderful day."

"I agree, Chef Tomas."

Seeing him smile is becoming more of a common occurrence since his father moved away.

"Mom ... about Jessica Stafford."

"Yees?"

"I'll say this about her — If I had to pick someone to have a crush on in my class, it would probably be her. She only lets her friends call her Jess, and I call her Jess. She's brilliant, independent, a complex thinker like I am, and she doesn't take 'no' for an answer. I like her, but she's so demanding."

"How is she demanding?"

"No matter what I do or say, she seems annoyed or disappointed with me. That's how TCC treated me, so why would I want more of that and coming from a girl. Forget it. I'm not interested in her after all."

"Have you spoken to her about the way she treats you?"

"There's no point; she already has a boyfriend who's in a military academy. He's everything I'm not, talk about intimidating. My life is way too complicated as it is."

"I understand. Maybe there's someone else who'd take less work?"

"That's a thought. I might like Maarlee McGee then. You know her, right? The one with the most popular show?"

How intriguing, my son is attracted to strong women. That means he sees me as strong. I guess I've come a long way.

"Maarlee would qualify as low maintenance because she's always somewhere on planet Earth; I wouldn't have to be with her that often."

"I can relate to that," I say, subtly referring to his father.

He shifts subjects, "Mom, I can't go into a lot of details, but I'm working on a project with Jess, top secret. I've brought Dahvid in too."

My heart is swelling with pride, knowing that Tomas is collaborating with Jessica, crush aside. Dahvid, Anamaría's son, is a wonderful and accomplished young man. The more time they spend together, the better.

"Mom, I need to ask you … Based on your own experience as a teenager..." He looks straight at me. "You were a teenager at some point, right?"

Another chance to hear myself laugh out loud.

"Yes, my dear, teenagers existed way back when. We were different because we didn't have technology implanted inside our bodies from age six like you or from birth like younger children. We were just regular kids trying to figure things out."

"Right, I remember when you told me that once before, it makes more sense now."

He's getting a bit twitchy, so he stands up to walk around the kitchen. He's either finding the courage to ask something challenging or looking for the right words to express his ideas.

"Please wait for me to ask all questions before answering." He instructs with a tone I wish he hadn't inherited.

I nod so as not to interrupt his thinking process.

"One, what would it be like if we could navigate the world propelled by our own hormones, with our own emotions, without depending on our implants or the Intellitela?"

"Wow, that's a great question, lots of … oops." I blurt out.

"Please, Mom, follow my instructions! Don't interrupt."

He stomps his foot on the floor. What a funny move for him to make.

"Sorry, Tomas." I cover my smile with the napkin.

"Two, are we currently being held hostage by our devices?"

"Three, would we feel freer if we could read our own natural signals without depending on these devices?"

"Ok, mom, that's it. You may answer in any order you like. I'll sort it out. Think about it. I'll be back in thirty."

Clearing the table, I realize I've only dared discuss similar questions with a few trusted colleagues, behind closed doors, for fear of retaliation from The WLC. Our children have become walking, talking laboratories. Their implants are being disabled for no good reason, making them feel like 'out of date' discarded devices. If only I could tell Tomas to hang in there. We're so close to recreating the atmosphere of other planets in the lab to find ways for kids to function freely and without technology.

I sit on the sofa and drift off, reliving the joy of experiencing my children laughing and joking. A delightful scent brings me back.

"Hi, Tomas." The scent is aftershave.

"Thought you were getting ready for bed. I see you're wearing a whole new outfit."

"I think more clearly wearing certain colors, and since we have a teleconference with Jess later, I must be focused."

I'm going to pretend this is his first date. He probably doesn't realize how great he looks, especially in that color. My boy is turning into a handsome young man with chiseled looks and piercing hazel eyes.

"I'm ready for you, sir, let's get started. Full disclosure, before we begin, these answers are based on my personal beliefs; they are not a common practice. I don't want you quoting me. Understand?" I insist.

"That's why I like you, Mom; you're an original. You have my word, I just need this to propel my research."

"Alright, son, here's my take. From a biochemical standpoint, hormones regulate everything in our bodies. Because of that, humanity has been held hostage by hormones from the beginning of time. We make decisions based on our endocrine system. Do we feel calm or nervous when we make decisions or when we're with certain people? Are we attracted to them, do we fear them, should we marry them, or have children with them?"

I stop myself — my answers went in the wrong direction, I'm revealing too much.

"Are you okay Mom? You don't look so good all of a sudden. Was it the food you ate or the subject matter?"

"I'm okay, honey, definitely not the food."

He offers me a sip of water. "On a broader scale, peaceful times show a balance of estrogen and testosterone, whereas, in wartime, there's an excess of testosterone. Those are the times of darkness in the world."

"You mean like now, right?"

"Exactly! Right now, we're experiencing major changes, but with them comes tremendous creativity, scientific advance, phenomenal talent in music, like yours, fabulous art, and so on."

"Then that explains why Sahrit Bana is so accomplished, she's only fourteen." He jumps in.

"I agree, she's incredible. Now, what I'm about to tell you is legitimately top-secret."

"Say more." He leans in.

"The Chancellor refused the activation of his implants."

"What? Could anyone have chosen to do that?" Tomas leans in more, resting his elbows on the table. This color really does help his ability to focus. I would have 'lost him' by now.

I continue to share, "To remain a dominant and powerful man, he's chosen to live in isolated darkness and he's forcing others into becoming just like him."

"But why?"

"He only recognizes data when he sees it through the lens of extreme contrast; otherwise, he's not able to differentiate those who oppose him. This man is incredibly insecure and threatened by any light emanating from the world. Do you know what kind of light I'm referring to?" I ask.

"I ... think ... I ... do." He replies slowly as he processes.

"That's why this man is especially bothered by kids, you're very smart and aware of everything going on around you. You're full of light and hope for the future. He can't stand that and that's why he refers to all of you as Hybrids."

Tomas is listening intently, and by his expression, I can tell he's connecting the dots to his father's behavior.

"Implants were designed by worldwide scientists, united by a common goal. They wanted to help balance the many signals that fire off randomly in our bodies. They wanted to help children have happier lives and not depend so much on medications for learning differences or anxiety attacks. Most importantly, they continue finding ways to prevent us from falling victim to future pandemic viral takeovers."

"So, what changed. Why are adults taking sides with him?"

"Parents were convinced that without implants, their children would fail at managing life. They forgot that they did just fine without them for millennia. It's a matter of perspective, we always want to improve on what we have but sometimes inventions can ..."

"... Go terribly wrong, right, like with me?" Tomas states, looking defeated.

"No, son, they didn't go wrong for you, it's that you need more adjustments than the average kid. You're my brilliant, beautiful, very complicated boy and you're far from average." I start tearing up.

"Don't be upset, Mom, you've just gifted me with life-altering insights."

He puts his right cheek against my left. That's as close to kissing as he can come. I don't usually hug or kiss him except in extreme cases, for fear of upsetting him further. He does allow me to rub his head and neck when he needs help winding down to go to sleep. He becomes a docile puppy dog. Maddy, of course, loves physicality, which is great for me as her mother but concerning because of her need for attention from boys.

"Mom ... we should collaborate on an invention. Imagine people literally putting their heads together, like this. We could transfer ideas, knowledge, personality traits, feelings without speaking."

He pauses and closes his eyes, smiling ear to ear.

"Imagine ... living in a world of nonverbal communication."

I melt.

"Good night Mom."

"Goodnight my beautiful boy."

He walks towards his room with a newly found rhythm to his step. I rest my elbows on the table, weave my fingers together, and lean my forehead against them as tears of relief roll down my face. If living with coldness and disdain was necessary to produce these two wonderfully fascinating children, then so be it.

Tomas closes the door gently behind him and starts dictating …

Welcome To The Great Unknown
By Tomas Kesher

In normal times, I'd be going to The Recalibration Center within three months of my fourteenth birthday for an implant adjustment. Would I have to report that playing guitar and percussion resolved more issues than the technology implanted in my body eight years ago? Does playing help because I feel empowered holding a magnificent instrument, or is it that I need the power of the electricity surging through my body?

Once the implants are disabled, how will I feel in a completely natural state of 'being' and in a natural state of adolescence? I've never 'been' there before. Will we be living in constant fear, eventually becoming the new normal? Constant fear is my normal, so what will change?

My existence requires a form of voluntary quarantine. It protects me from the harsh reality of living on this planet. The only time I feel in control is in the music studio. That's when I'm fully integrated and connected, with no judgments or distractions from anyone or anything. Cells and neurons unite as one, and as one, my 'being' feels settled.

I have been directed towards this otherworldly form of self-expression. The effects produced by each musical composition is essential to my survival. There is a steep price to pay for this gift. A single note may not go to waste, nor may it be directly absorbed by anyone else around me. That single precious vibrational molecule would take away from my daily sustenance needed to remain on Earth. Providing moments of pure ecstasy for others would inevitably subtract time from my existence.

My assigned costume on this planet makes me appear awkward, overly sensitive, antisocial, rigid, and phobic. On the other hand, people perceive me as extremely talented in tech and a pure genius on guitar and percussion. The multidimensional language designed by 'Phire' transcends words, creating every feeling ever felt.

This language expresses the universal anguish humanity keeps inside. I feel that some unknown force is registering our communal desperation, one that is capable of great compassion. This force is waiting patiently, willing to help. If only we knew how to ask for what we need. If only we knew what we needed.

Where is this very real and essential feeling coming from? Is it meant to be private or shared?

Is this burgeoning spirituality I feel forming within my earthly vessel?

Holding his sapphire blue electric guitar with a new firm stance, Tomas senses that its weight is balanced for the very first time. He feels empowered with fuel from freshly acquired insights. All energy and focus funnel into the most crucial piece of technology he'll ever own.

With eyes closed, the coding begins.

Colorful streams and swirls appear, manifesting as Fibonacci Spirals finding an escape route through that undetected fracture in the window. The one that appeared years ago, when Tomas spoke up for the first time.

His message will soon find its way to where he's fully understood, guaranteeing him a most extraordinary life ...

Cast

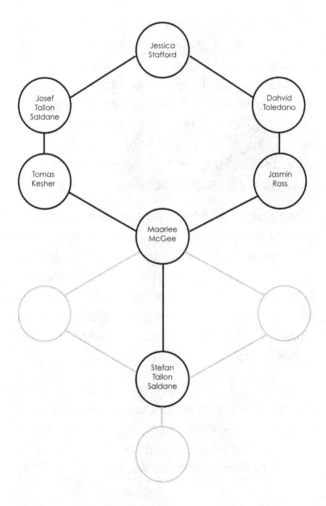

Acknowledgments

As very private people, unused to speaking about ourselves, we're doing just that, through the characters in Liberty 2041. We decided to explore our own lives and our observations of the world to weave a tapestry of relatable and interesting characters. Through them, we're expressing a commonality of dreams, humor, likes, dislikes, fears, and triumphs. We are forever fascinated with human behavior.

When Robert and I first met in early December of 2017, it took only a few days to recognize we were designed for each other. We felt that strong connection seen in movies or read about in books. We validated each other's impressions of what it's like to live in a world of extroverts while being creative introverts, empaths, and highly sensitive people.

Love for art, architecture, interior design, music, literature, and theatre blended with biology, archeology, psychology and a later in life understanding of spirituality, molded us to be the perfect fit we are for each other. This same eclectic combination of interests lead each of us to create and develop 'out of the ordinary' professions which also happen to blend perfectly. Robert became an Ontologist, author, and inventor of an intuitive system that connects implanted nanotechnology with feelings, sensations, colors, etc.

As an Interior Designer, I was inspired to develop a specialty revolving around sensory overload. Once I realized I possessed a fascinating neurological phenomenon called Synaesthesia which allows me to taste colors, see sounds, and so on, my practice took a very different direction.

We are convinced that we've been brought together for many reasons. Bringing this series to light is one of the main ones.

The manuscript for Liberty 2041 was written by Robert in 2014. After we married, he discovered my inherited love for writing and a great desire to write a book about my perception of the world.

We are so excited to join forces to bring you an interesting story about special kids with very special talents. Their goal, much like ours, is to be understood by bringing about a world of positivity and beauty. Our stories are meant to reassure children of all ages that uniqueness is indeed a gift, one to be nurtured and treasured. We feel we were brought together to transform the lives of others. We want to be inspiring and motivating, we want to help you accomplish things you never thought possible.

Robert, it's thrilling to have finally met you and to be your wife. You are a wonderful father to your sons. Thank you for placing before me yet another venue in which I can be creative and express myself in so many new ways. I love you. Co-authoring this incredible manuscript, where much of our work comes to fruition, only proves how soul mates can be in communication without knowing it. Our paths have crossed many times in different ways and knowing we were living a mile apart for so long, is a story in itself.

With deep love and eternal gratitude to my beautiful (inside and out) talented mother, best friend, Helene Silverman, raised by a young widowed mother of four in a small southern town. This brilliant young woman, graduated high school at age sixteen with a full scholarship. Loving books made her a prolific writer and prepared her to become an English and Phonetics teacher to Latin American students. She was also an integral part of the team who developed the original ESL Program in UT Austin. She led her life with unbounded love and ferocious loyalty towards her family and friends. Her passion for the arts, her great sense of humor with perfectly timed sarcasm, her innate talent for design, her sense of whimsy, her ability to write, have all contributed to my own tapestry. I love her and miss her beyond all words. Her influence is always with me. It's clear that she and Robert would get along beautifully because they are so much alike in many ways.

To her two closest friends, Graciela, a petite and feisty 'citizen of the world' of Hungarian parents who fought passionately for everyone's rights while being up on the latest fashion trends. Silvia, a determined Italian born artist who established an art school for children. She gave talented shy children in Mexico City a voice in which to express ourselves through non-verbal communication. How fortunate to have had a mother with great friends who inspired and loved me.

To the innumerable design clients, I've had and continue to have in my ever-evolving career. Thank you for trusting my intuition and being living testimonials that my version of Interior Design is not just a thing of beauty but truly a healing art. Much of what I have learned and developed is reflected in this series of stories.

Robert's childhood in Dallas made him feel constantly judged and misunderstood because he was bright beyond his years. Some of what he could do defied all explanation since he was too young to read instructions. When he was old enough to learn about the works of Albert Einstein, he finally found a brilliant man to identify with. When this active little boy wasn't reading, he was playing with his neighborhood friends. When he needed solace during difficult times, he'd climb trees to gain focus and strength to persevere. To this day, he admires trees in all their majesty and likes pointing out what makes some ideal for kids to climb.

His instinct has always been to seek truth and light over darkness.

His first female mentor was no exception. This lovely woman and her husband, lived up the street with their seven children. Their last name was Leicht (pron. light) and her first name was Faith. Robert enjoyed being around them as often as possible. She introduced him to spirituality, the many aspects of generosity, and above all, empathy. She saw him for who he really was, a sweet, loving gifted little boy who needed nurturing and encouragement to develop to his full potential.

During life's journey, Robert met Fernando Flores in January 1982. This Chilean born, world-renowned Ontologist enabled Robert to be granted a full scholarship for three years to study Ontology by his side. This opportunity along with the works of the ontological designer, Brian Regnier eventually lead to Robert's invention. This system that could come after the Internet, promises to protect one's privacy while expanding capacities to relate to ourselves and others.

Thank you to Brooke Falls, Jasmine Thompson and their supportive parents for their insights on being young talented musicians. Much was learned through your hopes and expectations for the future.

For my sons, Barrett and Spencer — Working from home allowed me to enjoy every phase of your development to the fullest. You taught me much more than I ever taught you. I love being your Pops.

For my wife, Carolyn — I'd be remiss if I didn't express that our relationship empowers me ever so completely. Even though I never met your mom, I experience her as being a very important part of my life. I've always thought of myself as being spiritual but couldn't explain it until we met. Now, looking back, I realize that I've been guided and cared for all my life. Through our bond and our desire to learn, a mystical world is being revealed before us. Liberty 2041 is a way to express our findings as they come together with human nature and science.

Carolyn, I love you and our partnership in all aspects of life. You are my brilliant, talented, artistic Princessa who has blessed my life beyond the joys of being a parent. Now that my two sons have become incredible men in their own right, you have filled that hollow that comes from not having them close by. Though we come from different backgrounds, you and I share the same aspirations and the same principles. We feel the same way about respect and dignity for others. There is no way I could have ever imagined being so perfectly matched.

As a couple, we'd like to thank all the children and teens we are friends with. We enjoy playing and interacting with you. We love you and consider it a priviledge to learn so much from seeing the world through your eyes.

To our family and friends that have become our family, our sincere gratitude for your support throughout the years. For the loving prayers and encouragement that made it possible for us to not give up until we found our match.

Finally, to Lyda Mclallen, our co-editor, publisher, and marketer, for expressing an immediate interest in our series. For encouraging us to express our life's philosophy; one where children are heard and respected and never labeled. For finding it refreshing to have a book filled with naiveté.

We're so excited to see our first born materialize in this first book.

About the Authors

Carolyn and Robert Gold

Authors, Carolyn and Robert first met in 2017. It only took them a few days to realize they were designed for each other. They had that intense and mysterious connection we see in movies and read about in books.

Their chemistry was instant.

The author's eclectic combination of interests had led each of them to create and develop 'out of the ordinary' professions on their own. Now that they're together, they complement each other perfectly. Robert became an Ontologist, author and inventor of an intuitive system that connects implanted nano technology with feelings, sensations, colors, etc.

As a classically trained Interior Designer, Carolyn developed a unique specialty addressing focus and sensory overload. Her muse, a neurological phenomenon which allows her to see sounds, hear sights, taste colors, etc. Though unfamiliar with Synesthesia before they met, Robert, inexplicably, had recreated the experience through nano technology.

As co-authors, they are combining their experiences and skills to write an episodic series called Liberty 2041.

9 781952 998003